Shopping for an Heir

by Julia Kent

Gerald Wright works for billionaires. He never imagined he'd become one.

The former Navy Seal is a chauffeur by day, artist by night, so when hotter-than-ever ex-fiancée Suzanne Dayton interrupts his nude model sculpting class to serve him with inheritance paperwork from a man he's never heard of, he assumes it's a joke.

Turns out the joke's on him. There's just one catch. A big one.

And it might be Suzanne—in more ways than he ever dreamed.

Shopping for an Heir is the 10th book in the New York Times bestselling Shopping for a Billionaire series by Julia Kent. It features many favorite characters from the Shopping series, including Declan McCormick himself as Gerald's class model ;)

TABLE OF CONTENTS

PRAISE FOR JULIA KENT

FROM AUTHORS

"Only Julia Kent could have me laughing my socks off one minute and reaching for the tissues the next. A laugh out loud, wild Vegas wedding adventure!"—Daisy Prescott, *USA Today* bestselling author

"This one has it all: hilarious laughs, a sexy (almost) billionaire and a hint of tears. The best of the series!"
—Celia Kyle, *New York Times* bestselling romantic comedy author

"Julia Kent's romantic comedies are so funny you'll snort soda out your nose, so emotionally honest you'll get misty eyed, and so charming you'll be back for more. Loved the whole series!"
—Cheri Allan, author of the *Betting on Romance* series

READER REVIEWS

"You can see that he really loves Shannon to the very core of his soul, and it's beyond interesting to watch how that love can bring a strong, confident, alpha male like Declan to his knees."

"Wonderful laugh out loud story of a family that reminds me of my own. I'm a sucker for good 'how they met' stories, and this is is by far the most creative. I wholeheartedly recommend you read the series."

"Every chapter made my heart beat faster in anticipation. Julia Kent once again pulls at our emotions and allows us to fall in love with the characters all over again.… Very well worth my heart palpitations."

"If I could describe this book in a word, it would be, 'EVERYTHING'.

It has everything you want in a romance.

It has those witty and sometimes downright hysterical situations that you can't help but laugh at.

It has those hot, sexy moments that make a romance book a, well, hot and sexy romance book.

It has all those quirky, fun characters we've all come to enjoy through this series.

But better than all that, it has what I loved best about this book: those sweet, tender expressions of love that are written so beautifully and artistically."

"As an avid reader I have to say there is nothing better than an author that can combine romance and humor. Julia never disappoints, and is one of the best at creating stories that suck you in and keep you laughing."

READER EMAILS

"I just can't imagine how you come up with this stuff, but am so glad you do!"

"I finally had to write to you and tell you that you are simply one of the most amazing authors. Your humor is perfect. I really do bust out laughing out loud. My family thinks that I am crazy when I do it but I can count on a good read from you especially when it has been a rough day. There hasn't been a single thing that you have written that I haven't fallen in love with the characters. They become real and some of your lines have become a part of our family language. Thank you for sharing your amazing gift."

"Having another fantastic evening as I just finished your latest book and now the fam can go to sleep since the laughing/screaming out loud has stopped... Stomach muscles are sore. Better than sit-ups! :-)"

ACKNOWLEDGEMENTS

To Daisy, for helping me understand how rare artifacts work in the auction and fine art business.

To Maria, who tirelessly puts up with my shenanigans and who has a sense of humor I appreciate deeply.

To long ago high school classmates who really did get duped once, and who (indirectly) helped me to think up a certain scene.

To "Clark," my husband, for taking me out to dinner on our wedding anniversary and helping me to come up with one of the funniest scenes in this book.

To my secret beta readers (you know who you are!), thank you for all your help.

To my Facebook reader group, *Laugh Your Way to Love*, for your never-ending support.

And to all who have served in the armed forces, from family members of my own to readers and beyond. Your sacrifices are much appreciated, and I thank you.

SHOPPING FOR AN HEIR

CHAPTER ONE

"You promised me a naked hot young man, and you'd better deliver on that promise, Mr. Clean."

Gerald Wright wasn't quite sure he'd really heard that. Did the sweet old lady who wore sequined white tennis shoes that matched her pink cardigan really say—

"I didn't pay $149 for this art class to play with pears and apples and make ashtrays out of clay. I want some man candy to ogle."

Oh yeah. Heard it loud and clear.

Gerald Wright looked up slowly from his clipboard, eyelids in place, eyeballs doing the work as he met the steely glare of a woman old enough to have voted for Roosevelt.

Maybe even *Theodore* Roosevelt.

"Class doesn't start for five minutes, ma'am. Cool your jets." He took a good look at her. He'd seen holy men in Afghanistan with fewer wrinkles. Eyes sunken deep into weathered flesh, she had a twisted, puckered mouth, moved with slow intent, and wore a pink t-shirt with white lettering across the chest that said, "My Breasts Used To Be This High."

Without thinking, he looked down and saw that along the hemline the shirt said, "Ha! Made You Look."

He cringed.

"I haven't had to cool my jets in forty years. My jet hormones left along with all my tight skin," she said, jiggling her arms. The woman had *batwings*.

Gerald nearly ducked.

"Agnes!" Another older woman appeared behind the old lady, hobbling on a metallic walker with yellow tennis balls covering the front two posts. She wore a blonde wig with feathered hair. Gerald tried not to do a double take, because the wig looked exactly like hair from that old '70s show, *Charlie's Angels*. Bright red lipstick completed the look.

"Quit pestering the nice young man." She stopped and gave Gerald a once over. "You look like Kojak."

Agnes blinked hard. With no eyelashes, she looked like a baby bird. A very wrinkled, ornery baby bird with a mouth like a sailor. "He doesn't look like Kojak! Get with the program, Corrine. Kojak sucked on a lollipop. This one looks like that other bald actor."

Gerald ran a palm against his shaved head and tried not to groan. He searched the class list. Yup. There they were: Agnes Duchamp and Corrine Morris.

And the magic words: Paid. In. Full.

It was going to be a long eight weeks.

"What other bald actor?" Corrine asked, squinting. She flashed Gerald a great big flirty smile, so full of life he couldn't help but smile back.

"You know. The one in that movie about the boy who saw dead people."

"Casper?"

"No."

"The two of them at the pottery wheel, having sex?"

"No."

"The one who was the captain of that new *Star Trek* show?"

"No."

"Agnes, I don't have all day to sit here playing Celebrity Alzheimer's with you. Which bald actor does this art teacher—what's your name?" Corrine pursed her lips as she asked the unexpected question, making Gerald sigh.

12

"Gerald. Gerald Wright."

"Gerald!" Agnes laughed. "What kind of name is that for a bald sculptor? Sounds like an accountant."

"Don't blame me, ma'am. My parents picked it."

"They must be wildcats. What'd they name your sister? Iphigenia?"

He opened his mouth to defend Victoria, his BASE-jumping, outdoor-survivalist-instructor little sis, but stopped himself.

"Like you should talk, *Agnes*," Corrine snapped, pointing at her friend. "People with old lady names shouldn't cast stones."

Agnes scowled, layers of skin folding in on each other, like origami. "What actor does he look like?" Agnes demanded of her friend, who reached up to her ear and fiddled with her earring, giving Gerald another bright smile he couldn't help but return.

"What?" Corrine asked Agnes sweetly.

"What actor does Gerald the Accountant look like?"

"What?" Corrine began moving like a turtle on speed toward the front of the room. A bumper sticker wrapped around one of the posts of her walker said, *I Brake for Naked Hitchhikers with Guitars.*

"Damn it, Corrine, you turned off your hearing aid again, didn't you?"

"What?" Corrine winked at him.

He was starting to like her.

"You're lucky you're still recovering from that surgery, Corrine, or I'd punch you."

"You punch me, and I won't share my lorazepam with you for those long weekends when your son-in-law comes to visit. You know. The one who wants to put you in a home?"

Agnes shut up.

As the two old ladies took their places in the front row, at the table directly before the model's platform,

Gerald greeted incoming students. So many new faces. He was lucky to get eight students per class, but tonight's roster showed twenty-seven.

The new marketing intern in the office was doing a bang-up job.

Woman after woman, most of them over fifty, began to assemble, buzzing with excitement, taking their places at the carefully spaced tables in the room.

"Gerald!" Stacy, one of the other interns in the art center's office, waved to him from the doorway. "You need more chairs? We have some walk-ins."

"Walk-ins? We never have walk-ins." Gerald strode across the room as the women in the front row hissed at each other under their breath, some kind of argument brewing.

"We do today!" Stacy had a high, squeaky voice when she was excited, a mouth full of braces, and more freckles than common sense. She was a good kid, twirling her blonde ponytail, eyes wide with an eagerness to please. "I think the total will come close to thirty."

"Then we need more sculpting clay."

"Want me to check the inventory?" she begged, eager for responsibility.

He grinned. "Of course. Couldn't pull this off without your help." The dazzling smile she returned cut quickly as she pivoted and sprinted down the hall to the supply room.

Thirty students. He hadn't taught thirty students all year, across four different sessions, for this Nude Sculpting class. What was going on?

Puzzled, he walked back into the room, a short line forming before him as people registered, by turns nervous and calm, some in pairs with a buddy, most of them seeming to know old Agnes and Corrine up there in front.

He narrowed his eyes and strode with purpose to the two of them, catching the end of a fevered conversation between Agnes and a fifty-something brunette.

"I've seen his ass before. Touched it, even," Agnes insisted.

"Class was supposed to start two minutes ago, and no Declan McCormick, Agnes. If I gave up my Tuesday night Wine and Whine Book Club because of you and there's no cute butt guy, you're toast."

"What are you going to threaten me with, Pauline? I'm ninety-three. Nothing scares me."

Corrine whispered, "Your son-in-law. Nursing home." She rolled her eyes. "And you're ninety-two, Agnes. For God's sake, can't you keep track?"

Agnes turned the color of a sheet.

"I'm not sure which one pisses me off more. My son-in-law or realizing I've been telling the world I'm a year older than I really am."

Corrine just shook her head and began making what looked like a penis out of the lump of modeling clay in front of her.

"Declan's coming. Don't worry," Agnes insisted, standing her ground, eyeing Corrine's sculpture with interest.

Gerald sighed, crossing his arms over his chest, clipboard bouncing in one hand as he tapped it against his biceps.

"You're quite the maven, aren't you, Agnes?"

"Maven?"

"Someone who spreads the word. Information broker."

"Been called worse," she cackled.

"You told all these women to come because of Declan McCormick's naked body?"

"Yes." She stared at him like the female version of Clint Eastwood in a *Dirty Harry* movie. Gerald stared back. A grudging respect began to grow in him. She was hard core.

"The Westside Center for the Arts thanks you," he replied, not breaking steely eye contact. "We've been trying to grow our classes."

"Get some hot nude models, then."

"That's not the purpose of these classes, ma'am."

"Purpose, schmurpose. You want more people like me, with disposable income and nothing more exciting at home than reruns of *To Catch a Predator* and videos on how to make gluten-free cauliflower pizza crusts on cable television to come to these classes, you spice them up."

"This is nude-model sculpting, designed to teach basic artistic anatomy. We're not here to titillate."

She reached into her purse and pulled out a flask. "Call it what you want, Gerald the Accountant. This is like the bachelorette party I never had."

And with that, Agnes sucked down a shot of whatever was in that flask.

Corrine reached for it. "Give me a nip."

"What?"

"I said, give me a nip."

Agnes' mouth twisted with a grin. "What?" She pointed to her ear and said, "Two can play that game, Corrine." She guzzled the rest of whatever liquid joy was in there.

It was going to be a *glacial* eight weeks.

Stacy jogged into the classroom, carrying a massive tub of modeling clay, face flushed, the hair around her scalp damp with sweat. "Here you go."

"Hey." The rumble of a man's baritone made all the sopranos and altos come to a halt. Gerald looked up.

Declan McCormick was finally here.

"I am late because I don't have a chauffeur anymore," he said pointedly, making a face. That was as close to an apology as the class would get out of the man. "Do you know how time-consuming parking in one of those garages can be? They make you walk to a pay station and walk back to your car with the ticket." He let out an exasperated sigh. "I don't know how people live like this. What a waste of time."

The room broke out in spontaneous applause.

Agnes got to her feet and turned around, facing her classmates, arms in the air like Rocky after defeating Apollo Creed. "See? Told you he'd be here."

Declan's eyes darted to the old lady, then rolled so high they might as well be cherry pickers. "Oh, God. Are you sure we're not in Salem? Because I see a witch."

"I see you've met Agnes," Gerald said, smothering a grin. He reached out to give Declan's hand a shake, the two pumping arms madly, women in the room sighing loudly.

"We're *intimately* acquainted," Agnes crowed proudly, then hiccuped. The crowd erupted into titters.

Declan pulled him in for a half hug. "Watch the fingers," he whispered. "She's more nimble than you think."

"Is that why enrollment's triple the norm? Word got out you're the model?"

Dec shakes his head. "Marie."

"Your mother-in-law is crazy."

"Tell me something I don't know."

"I know a lot about your family that *you* don't know." Because Declan no longer worked for Anterdec, their relationship had changed. He wasn't Gerald's boss anymore. Two months ago, he married Shannon and bought his own chain of coffee shops. Gerald still worked for Declan's brother, CEO Andrew, and their

17

father, James, who founded Anterdec more than thirty years ago.

"If you've got good dirt on my brother, I need to know."

"Non-disclosure agreement." He almost called him *sir*, but caught himself. "Sorry, Declan."

Oblivious to the twenty-seven sets of eyes on him, Declan took stock of Gerald. He knew how the guy worked. This was banter, word play, a man's-man kind of joking around.

"Fight you for it."

See?

"What're the terms?"

"Pool. Two out of three games. You win, you get me as a nude model for every class. I win, you give me one juicy detail about my brother. Something actionable."

Having a set model for every class would make the sessions flow better, and allow Gerald to get into advanced sculpting techniques. On the other hand, he liked having varying models. Light, shadow, contour, and all the finer points of sculpture could be assessed and taught with variation.

"I'll pay extra if he's the class model for all eight weeks!" crowed Agnes.

Murmurs of furious assent filled the room.

"You better be good at billiards, Mr. Clean!" Corrine chimed in.

"Mr. Clean?" Declan's eyebrow went up.

"Keep that face. I want it like that for the entire hour pose."

One side of Declan's mouth twitched, but he kept the perfect arch.

"Ladies! Ladies! Let's get down to business."

"I thought you were!" Agnes gave him a creepy smile. "You'd better be good at stripes and solids, mister.

My husband was a pool shark. Too bad he's dead, or he'd teach you a few things."

Declan walked through a small door right behind the instructor's platform.

"Where's he going?" Corrine asked sweetly. All the heads in the class turned to track him. It was like watching sunflowers follow the sun.

"To get ready," Gerald said, setting down his clipboard and looking out at the sea of faces. What a boon.

And as a matter of fact, he was a damn fine pool player.

Shark, even. That's how he made some extra money in high school.

Play stupid and let people underestimate you.

Then you have them at an advantage.

Declan emerged wearing a plain white bathrobe. The room filled with whispers.

"Welcome!" Gerald clapped his hands once, bellowing out the word. The commanding voice got their attention, heads swiveling toward him. They wore smocks and poked at the clay in front of them, uncertain but eager. Half the women looked at Declan like they were here for an appetizer rather than a lesson, but that was his model's problem.

Gerald was here to teach.

"I'm Gerald Wright, your instructor. Before you at each student's place, you'll find the necessary supplies for all eight classes, including a folder. Please take the notecard inside, fold it in half, and write your name on one half, facing it toward the front of class. Normally, we introduce ourselves, but the class is so big that we'd lose an entire session, so let's use name tags and go from there."

For the next two minutes, students shuffled notecards and pens, writing and folding, until all twenty-seven had little inverted Vs on their tables.

He walked in front of Declan, who now sat on his posing stool, still berobed.

Declan was frowning.

"What's wrong?" Gerald asked.

Following the billionaire's gaze, he quickly got the lay of the land.

Twelve women had written their phone numbers on their cards, instead of their names.

"Fascinating, ladies," Gerald said dryly. "So many of you have the first name 617. Must have been popular sometime in the early 1960s."

The laughter that filled the room was genuine.

One minute later, actual names were on the cards, and Gerald got down to business.

"Unlike most classes, we don't spend our first day learning theory. We dive right in."

Someone in the back whistled.

"This isn't a Pats game," Gerald said.

"Hope not! Don't need to see any deflated balls," Agnes cracked.

Declan's face was stone.

"Or a Red Sox game," Gerald said, trying to change the subject.

"You got a Green Monster under that robe?" Agnes asked Declan, grinning madly.

"What does that even mean?" Declan hissed. He turned to Gerald. "And stop with the sports comments. I don't even want to know what she comes up with for hockey."

Agnes chortled.

Gerald had to get his class under control.

"Ladies!"

Someone in the back had just entered the room. Two guys cleared their throats meaningfully.

"And gentlemen," he added with a nod. The two guys took their seats and put on aprons.

"Welcome to Nude Sculpting 101. This is a class for beginners. That said," he continued, his voice growing firmer, "this is a class where respect for the model is Rule #1."

The tittering simmered down.

Gerald mustered his old commanding voice, the one he had eased out of himself for the past ten years. From the gleam in a few eyes, he'd need it more than he did when he was in the Navy.

"You will not make jokes about the model's body. If this were a female model, you would never dare. Why should it be different because it's a man?"

Agnes started to open her mouth. He spun on her, finger pointed, and before she could speak, barked, "That was a rhetorical question."

Her mouth snapped shut.

"We are here to be artists."

Someone sighed. It was a happy sound.

"We are here to learn to connect what the eyes see with what the hands do."

More sighs and a few uncomfortable looks.

"You will learn about shadow and curve, form and realism, and how to find the deeper eye within you that guides the body toward what it knows it can recreate from memory, from stored touch—"

A sound of appreciation between two black women who had been chattering in whispers almost made Gerald smile. They gave him their rapt attention.

"You are artists," he repeated. "Not office workers or retirees or stay-at-home parents or college students. In this class, ninety minutes a week, you are creators. You are visioneers. You are sensual and grounded in the core essence of what it means to be human. Your hands and arms will take what you know, what you see, and give it life through the clay."

Now he had them eating out of his hand. He paced in the space between Declan and the first row, eyes on the students as he walked back and forth, slowly, but with deliberation.

"Let's see what you find within yourselves, ladies and gentlemen. That's what art is—self-exploration through expression. Connection by touching others through the visual, the tactile. Welcome to the world of art. And our arts center thanks you—your tuition money helps fund arts programs for kids and seniors, so the enthusiastic attendance is a welcome sight."

He stopped and looked at all the faces.

"Let's begin."

As if on cue, Declan dropped the robe.

The class gasped.

Gerald grinned.

CHAPTER TWO

"I can do this," Suzanne Dayton muttered under her breath, standing outside the decrepit arts center, pacing back and forth, trying desperately to find her old military voice. More than ten years out of the Navy after a two-year stint, and that world was like a different lifetime. Three years of law school and seven years as a practicing attorney—now a full partner at one of Boston's best firms—and here she was, trembling with anxiety at the thought of walking into a nude sculpting class.

The nude part? No problem.

The class part? No problem.

The instructor? *Big* problem.

And what she needed to deliver to him?

"Oh, God," she groaned. "How did my life come to this?"

The paperwork had come through to her early last week, a simple bequest. Suzanne worked in estate law, and this kind of inheritance wasn't uncommon. A non-relative inheriting an object with meaning. Clear. Easy. A transaction that happened all the time.

But the combination of this artifact, the billionaire who left it to an heir, and the heir himself left Suzanne shaking and nervous, acting like a first-year law student before final exams.

When she'd opened the paperwork and seen the name Gerald Wright, she'd closed the papers quickly, shoved them into the envelope, and asked Letitia to get her a rescue latte. Life was too confusing to do it without proper caffeine levels in her bloodstream.

"Cool!" Letitia had said, grabbing her purse. "Now I have an excuse to try that new coffee shop. Mind if I go to Congress Street?"

That meant a walk across the big bridge.

"Why so far?" Suzanne had been distracted by the sound of Gerald's absence echoing in her head. Silence does, in fact, make a sound, she'd learned. It sounds a bit like your heart breaking, over and over, endlessly.

"Great new coffee shop. Hear it's totally worth it. And they sell macarons," Letitia added. She was such a closer.

"Sold. Get me my usual and a half dozen of the chocolate kind."

Letitia was off in a flash, all bright primary colors and big grins.

Suzanne had stared at the paperwork until it blurred.

No amount of coffee had helped, not even the orgasmic latte from Grind It Fresh! Stupid name for a coffee chain, but they could get away with it.

She would never drink any other chain's brew again.

"Letitia, can I ask you to serve these papers?" she'd asked, knowing the truth was buried on page five.

Letitia had pointed out the clause, eagle-eyed paralegal that she was. "Look, Suzanne. Right here. Says Suzanne Dayton must serve the papers." Letitia's brow had furrowed. "Why you?" Great at speed reading, she'd skimmed the document.

Suzanne had waited for it.

"The object in question is a what?" Letitia's eyes bugged out of her head. "A gold religious artifact worth how much?"

"Nearly nine figures. Less if melted down and sold for gold and jewels. The cultural implications of what's inside the figurine are what make it so valuable."

Letitia had let out a low whistle. "Mr. Gerald Wright is about to have one damn fine afternoon."

Suzanne let out a laughing groan.

Oh, Letitia.

If only you knew.

"I can't deliver it, though." She'd shook her head. "Not that I wouldn't like to. This would be like delivering the news that you won the Publisher's Clearinghouse Sweepstakes. Mr. Gerald Wright is going to love you forever, Suzanne."

Love you forever.

Right.

He'd said that before. So many times.

When Suzanne didn't answer, Letitia touched her arm. "Suz? You okay? Is something wrong with this case?"

How could she answer that?

He hadn't loved her forever, after all.

Giving Letitia a weak smile and grabbing her paperwork to bring home, brief bag stuffed to the gills, Suzanne had spent the better part of a week figuring out the simplest way to deliver the papers to Gerald, her ex-fiancé, without having any contact with him.

When the head of your firm says you need to deliver legal documents personally, you do it.

Now here she was, standing outside the Westside Center for the Arts, struggling to get up the courage to go inside. Damn it. She'd been able to command a team in Afghanistan, and now she couldn't do a simple inheritance delivery.

This was all about strategy. Do it in public. Do it somewhere she could escape from easily. Do it in a place where Gerald would be preoccupied and unable to follow her.

Not that she thought he would. The guy dumped her, after all. Ten years of questions, ten years of self-doubt, ten years of pain.

Ten years of heartache.

So why did a tiny part of her wish he would follow her?

"Pah!" she exclaimed, impatient with herself. "Just go in."

The building was ancient and smelled like chalk and burning hair, the scent of old educational institutions with radiators and structural problems. As she walked down the hallway, following the signs to the office, she smelled paint, turpentine, and heard children laughing. A quick peek in one classroom showed parents sitting behind toddlers, hands immersed in clay, all of them smiling.

Her heart tugged.

That should be her.

Squaring her shoulders, she shoved her emotions into a locked box and strode with purpose. Find the office. Locate Gerald. Serve the papers. Walk away.

Simple.

"Excuse me?" she asked, striding into a cluttered little office with desks that looked like something issued to an Afghanistan mobile unit. Suzanne paused. Nah.

These were older. *Much* older.

A fresh-faced blonde teenager looked up from her crouch, her face flushed with exertion, a pile of textured paper in her arms. "Yes?"

"I'm looking for Gerald Wright."

"Gerald's, um, teaching right now."

"Which room is he in?"

"Three thirteen."

"Thank you."

26

"But you can't just go in there!" the girl called out as Suzanne made her way to the stairs, mind nothing but the loop of the number, over and over.

Just keep moving forward.

"Miss!" the young girl said. "It's a closed class! Only enrolled students can go in there!"

Suzanne ignored her.

By the time she was at the top of the stairs, the girl had given up. One less obstacle. Who cared about enrolled students? Suzanne wasn't there to learn how to make a pear or form a horse head out of modeling clay. She knew Gerald must be teaching sculpture. The man lived for his art.

And those hands.

Oh, those hands of his.

"Stop it," she muttered to herself, pinching her wrist. "That will only get you into trouble."

Three eleven... three thirteen. She peered in through the wire-mesh-filled window and saw a packed class. Good for Gerald. She knew from a quick Google search (ok, more than a quick Google search...) that he worked in security for Anterdec, protecting the McCormick family men at Boston's famous Fortune 500 company. The art teaching must be on the side.

Standing before the door, she braced herself. Her legs began to tremble and below the calves, blood turned cold. She was wearing a work suit, heels, and had retouched her makeup before coming over.

None of that mattered if she couldn't move.

No one in the classroom talked. The angle of the door made it so she couldn't see Gerald, and there was a large curtain separating a small platform. She wondered what the subject was.

Should she knock?

No. Just do it. Be bold.

And so she was, opening the door, the *creeeeeak* of the un-oiled hinges announcing her arrival.

"Excuse me. Are you enrolled?"

Her knees melted. Gerald's voice could do that to her after all these years.

"Ah, no," she said, still unable to see him. All of the students whipped around in their seats, staring at her.

One step at a time, she told herself. Just one at a time.

"Then I'm afraid we're full, and—"

Gerald's words stopped as she came into view.

There is a point where looking at someone is like having all of the insides of your soul poured out onto an endless terrain of eternity, as if they use their eyes to pick you up and shake you hollow, all the pieces of yourself shining under an unrelenting sun without shadow.

Suzanne felt that once, ten years ago.

And again, now.

The point of contact between her and the man she'd loved so fiercely wasn't a tangent. There was no touch. Just eyes, the direct path of visual connection, the moment explosive and calm, like the eye of a tornado.

All the chaos inside her went impossibly still when he looked at her.

Just like that.

"Jesus. Suzanne? What are *you* doing here?" Gerald's voice went impossibly soft, his hands on his hips, a clipboard resting crooked in one hand, jutting out from his waist. Decorum said that gasping aloud at the sight of his chiseled form, the clay-smeared shirt conforming to the ridged muscle of his chest and belly, his faded jeans hanging on hips like they'd won a coveted spot, would not be the best approach right now.

And she was trying her best. Really.

28

He still shaved his head, and in that strange way that time changes when the mind needs it to, she wondered if he'd ever grown it out even as she knew she should say something. Anything. But her mind decided to take a detour, and she didn't have an emotional GPS that would reroute her appropriately right now. She was along for the ride.

Suzanne had seen pictures of his natural color, a wiry blond mane the color of ashes mixed with turmeric. But in their years together, she'd never run her hands through his hair, deprived of the simple luxury so casually taken for granted in most relationships.

Those eyes. As she moved beat by beat, time lost to emotion, she finally found herself looking at his face, the bones the same, his fierce handsomeness baked a bit by life. His nose was still crooked, broken long ago in his teen years. That nasty scar along the right side of his face, from earlobe to jaw, plagued her. She remembered when it was a fresh wound, the result of shrapnel from an IED. Now it was a thick white line marking time.

Time had filed off some of the hard corners, made him more approachable.

Shock and lust and joy and guardedness all stared at her through gemstone irises the color of the sky.

"Mr. Wright?" She used the title because she needed a boundary, no matter how invented.

Calm and cool, she took two more steps.

And froze.

Because just past Gerald, a vision of nude perfection stood on an elevated platform, a flesh-feast for the eyes, and Suzanne Dayton might have been nervous, but she wasn't *dead*.

"Oh," she said, her voice low and impressed by the class model, a man with dark green eyes, thick brown hair, and a chiseled body that made the David look kinda just okay.

You know.

Meh.

Skin not just kissed by the sun, but *French*-kissed with a reach-around thrown in for good measure, went on for miles. The man on the stage was tall and browned, muscles braided into cords that curled and straightened, tightened and loosened, the kinesthetic calibration a muscular symphony without sound. A feast for the eyes, and as he turned in place, she watched the domino effect of ribs and intercostal muscle rippling down his torso, the hypnotic effect triggering a deep ache.

And then she looked back at Gerald.

Who had never stopped looking at *her*.

The ache intensified.

"You two know each other?" Hot Nude Greek God Guy asked. He stood up from the stool on which he was perched and looked at her, then Gerald, his eyes filled with questions. Casual and comfortable, he had zero self-consciousness about being naked in a room full of more than thirty people.

She tried very, very hard not to look between his legs.

She failed.

"You're ruining the work, Declan! Sit down!" snapped an old lady in the front row. "Do you have any idea how hard it is to train my hands to manage an asymmetrical ball sac?"

"That's what she said," groaned someone from the back row.

"I like this view better," said another one, wearing a blond wig. "Stay right there. Everything dangles where it should be. By the time my husband was eighty, his balls were close to his knees."

The nude model took a step toward her, his body fluid and tight, all his skin drawn over compact muscle that looked like it belonged right where it was, exacting and calibrated. He had thick eyebrows, an expressive face, but one that stayed neutral now. She frowned, forcing herself to study his face after realizing she was a bit more consumed by observing the rest of him.

Declan.

Declan?

"Declan McCormick?" she gasped, the pieces fitting. "The Montgomery Trust? Anterdec?" Elena Montgomery had been married to James McCormick, and upon her death, her three sons had come into a substantial family trust, one that Suzanne helped to manage. Once a year, she met with the three McCormick sons.

She'd never seen Declan quite like *this* before.

Unable to stop herself, her eyes combed over the fine details of his cut body, the shoulders broad, arms toned as if sculpted by hands like Gerald's, the eight-pack of abs a work of art in flesh form. His waist narrowed to inverted Vs of muscle at the hips, a smattering of dark hair on olive-toned skin a delightful vision. The man was tanned, with thick thighs featuring an array of rippling muscle, hardened by years of exertion, graced by good bones and genes but maintained by sheer will and steady discipline.

She felt her mouth go dry and water at the same time.

Gerald moved with that bold swiftness she knew well, inserting himself between the nude model and her, reaching for her arm and pulling her toward the open classroom door. His touch electrified her, the sudden rush of her pulse sending blood through her like a sonic boom. Gerald smelled like clay and paint, with a faint undertone of sweat and coffee. If you added sand and sunshine, she'd think it was a decade past.

He smelled like home. Like love. Like promise and comfort, like passion and disbelief.

"What's wrong?" he snapped, his face alternating between joy and anger. "Why are you here?"

Coming to her senses, she extracted the thick envelope from her brief bag, looking him square in the eye. "Legal matter. I've been instructed to deliver this to you." She used remarkable restraint in not peering around Gerald to get more of an eyeful of Declan McCormick's stately form.

Then again, Gerald was an impenetrable wall of muscle himself, not easily subverted. She'd need taller heels to peer around him. He did not move his palm from her arm, and his touch infused her, a deeply satisfying sense of connection slowly creeping along her skin, her breath quickening, his touch ringing bells inside her that had been dormant for a decade.

"What is it?"

"Read it. You'll understand." She turned on her heel and started to leave, shaking inside so hard she might trigger the New Madrid fault.

He glared at her. "What? That's it? Ten years and that's it?" He pulled back, breaking contact.

All her anxiety faded, like an antidote injected straight into the heart, his words kicking in, providing such clarity.

"Ten years *you* chose, Gerald," she hissed, mouth curling, throat seizing. "You do not get to put this on me." Grief flared in her, a burst like a fireball, and then it turned to the ash of anger, a light coat settling over every spare surface of her heart.

His eyebrows shot up, eyes gliding away, his nose twitching and mouth tightening as if holding back.

Squaring her shoulders, Suzanne decided to make this easy for him. God only knew why. "My law firm is handling the estate of deceased billionaire Harold

Hopewell. You've been named in his will." She tapped the thick envelope in his hand. "These papers explain everything."

"Explain *what*?"

"You're his heir. One of them, at least."

At that moment, a leaky pipe released a drop that went *ker-plunk* into a ragged bucket on the floor.

"How can I be an heir to a guy I don't even know?" His words were about the dead billionaire, but she knew he was just trying to engage her. Make her stay.

She looked around. She had to get out of there. "Read the papers. If you have any questions, my office number is on the letterhead." Turning to go, she felt his gaze on her, like a touch.

"Suzanne." His voice was low and filled with ten years of yearning. "Please."

Please.

Of all the words she'd imagined Gerald saying to her when they finally saw each other again, that was the last one she'd ever expected to hear.

If she pivoted and caught his eye, she'd cry. Or scream. Or worse—stand there pleading with him to take her back, to undo ten years of heartache, to atone for the unspeakable pain of being unceremoniously dumped and left brokenhearted, shattered into a thousand pieces before she was stateside, left to unpack her meager civilian belongings in her parents' house in Minnesota and try not to talk about anything but her future.

Frozen, she stood a few feet from the doorway, the weight of her brief bag pulling on her shoulder, anchoring her in place. If he touched her again, she'd melt.

If he touched her again, she'd explode.

If she just stood there, letting her pulse pound through her like a helicopter blade whipping through too much thick wind, she would never move.

Slowly, with painstaking intent, she did swivel, her heels nearly choreographed for a dance she couldn't avoid. Meeting his eyes, she let herself feel all the emotions at once, uncensored, but only for a few seconds.

He didn't flinch. Didn't blink. Just met her look head-on, the power of seconds ticking by without reprieve from each other's look growing.

"Please what?"

"Please stay after class and talk with me."

"I can't," she announced in a firm voice. "I have a date."

Anger could do the most extraordinary things to eyes. She watched it fill his irises, clouds of ozone and shock stuffed into two orbs that looked at her through a furrowed brow.

"You know where to find me," she said, nudging her nose toward the thick packet in his hand. She made a huffing laugh. "Then again, you always have."

And with that, she took one very obvious gander at nude Declan McCormick, gave him a smile and a thumbs-up, and marched out of Gerald's class, down the hallway, and into the warm late-summer night.

It was all she could do not to scream.

CHAPTER THREE

Gerald willed his hands not to shake when he took the shot, sending a yellow-striped nine ball into the corner pocket, making him stripes, Declan solids.

"I have to hear this story," Declan said, watching as Gerald set up for his next shot.

"Ten in the left corner pocket," Gerald replied. Eyeing the shot, he lined up the cue, discerning the perfect angle, the exact spot on the table edge where he could get the ball's trajectory in alignment to go where his mind's eye saw it.

"How do you know Suzanne Dayton?" Declan asked, just as Gerald was taking the shot. He damn near ripped the table cover with a jagged push of surprise.

"How the hell do *you* know Suzanne?" Gerald growled, a burst of fire pulsing through him, heating his skin as he stopped breathing. If Declan ever dated her...

"Business."

Gerald inhaled.

"Her firm handles my mother's family trust. Once a year, we have a lovely two-hour meeting. She's been at the table for the past seven years. Junior associate at first, now full partner."

"Huh. Didn't know." How long had she been living in Boston? Gerald wondered. He'd forced himself, years ago, not to look her up. Other than knowing she'd gone to law school at University of Michigan, he'd let her go. It had been about eight years since he'd cracked open the door to that Pandora's box.

"You drove me nearly every time."

"Shit."

"I take it you two have a past."

Something like that.

Stalling, Gerald pointed his cue at Declan, who made a short shot quickly, the ball slamming into the center pocket. Bam bam bam—three balls in rapid-fire succession before Declan missed.

"Loser tells all," Declan declared.

Gerald grunted, then smiled. "Fine. I lose, I tell you about Suzanne. You lose, you tell me about your honeymoon."

Declan paled, his five o'clock shadow more pronounced, giving his face the look of a *Vogue* model. "I promised Shannon I'd never tell."

"Must have been one hell of a honeymoon."

Declan scratched the top of his thigh, then shook his head slightly, as if clearing a memory. "Yeah. Different bet, though. Can't talk about it. *Won't* talk about it."

The two squared off in a staring match, until Gerald relented. "Fine. Same rule applies to Suzanne." He took his shot.

Missed.

Damn it.

"You pinkie-promised never to discuss whatever happened?"

Gerald looked at Declan's manicured hands. "*Pinkie* promise?"

The guy rolled his eyes. "You know Shannon."

"Suzanne's not exactly the pinkie promise type."

"I got that impression. Tough as nails."

"Tougher. How about loser buys the next round?"

"You're on. She's your ex?"

Gerald sighed. Might as well get this out there. Being invited to go out for beer and pool by his former boss had been the cherry on top of a decidedly bizarre day. Revealing personal details about his life wasn't exactly his style.

And yet.

"We were engaged. Ten years ago."

Declan was about to take a shot when he paused, pulling the cue off the table, sending it upright with the rubber stopper on the floor. His eyebrows went up. "Engaged?" He blinked. "I take it you ended it."

"How'd you guess?"

He shrugged. "Pretty clear she's still in love with you."

Gerald damn near snapped his cue in half.

"What?"

When Declan McCormick smiled—the genuine grin of someone caught up in their own amusement—one side of his mouth moved up, making a deep dimple appear. Gerald noticed only because he heard Shannon McCormick comment on it often.

"It's obvious. I've met her before. She's stone-faced."

"Takes one to know one," Gerald muttered as Declan resumed his shot, flicking the green six ball into a side pocket like he was dispensing with a piece of lint on his cuff.

"And that," Declan said, clearly not offended by Gerald's comment, "is why I am qualified to know that she's still not over you." He gave Gerald an appraising look. "You must have something special for a woman like that to carry a torch."

"Nothing special." Gerald set up his shot. Three ricochets at perfect angles and he could blast a cluster of balls, sending one into a corner pocket. As he drew back the cue, the white end slipped between the index and middle fingers of his left hand, Declan spoke.

"My brother tried to date her once."

A long, thick line of blue chalk from the cue's tip left a ragged line on the brown table-covering, the shape not unlike a tube of lipstick dragged down a chalkboard.

The idea that Declan's brother Andrew, the current CEO of Anterdec, would even touch Suzanne's pinky finger filled Gerald with an unbridled rage that he could not quell.

"But she turned him down," Declan said casually, filling his mouth with the green end of a beer bottle, leaving Gerald a smoking piece of charcoal.

"Why?"

Declan shrugged. "Because she has taste?"

In damn near any other conversation about Andrew McCormick, Gerald would defend him.

Not this one.

"You didn't hit the ball, so technically it's your shot again," Declan pointed out, signaling the cocktail waitress by holding up two fingers, being gracious with the extra shot. Out of the corner of his eye, Gerald saw the waitress nod.

Gerald grunted.

"Try not to turn the table blue," Declan said with a snort. He leaned back against a table edge, crossed his jeans-covered legs at the ankles, and watched Gerald with a relaxed countenance he'd never seen in the man. Though he'd arrived for the nude sculpting class in a suit, he'd come out of the dressing area in clothes that were pretty damn close to what Gerald wore, except the t-shirt was free of clay.

The waitress brought two beers. Declan told her to start a tab.

"I'll get the next round," Gerald announced, pride kicking into full gear.

"You will when you lose," Declan said in a mocking tone, eyes all steel and challenge.

Gerald laughed, drawing on the same powers of concentration that had served him well as a sniper, and *bam!*

Cluster shattered.

Ball in the left side pocket.

Ball in the left corner pocket.

Too bad they were Declan's balls.

"Mmm," Declan muttered, throat working as he finished his cold beer. "Next one's going to taste so much better. Beer always does when someone else is buying."

A hush filled the bar suddenly, heads turning to watch the television. A bombing in Turkey. Another one in Kabul. Both claimed by the same terrorist organization.

Declan looked at the television politely, then returned to the game. "Weren't you in Kabul?" he asked, having no idea how loaded those words really were.

"Yes."

"With Suzanne?"

Gerald's back straightened slowly, like a snake rising up to look at its surroundings before striking.

"How did you know?"

"I didn't. Put two and two together. She mentioned serving in Afghanistan. Is that where you met?"

"For a guy who hates being asked about his personal life, you sure do ask a lot of questions, Declan."

He pulled up, dropping the cue to the floor, leaning on it. Assessment filled his eyes, which were shadowed by the strange bar lights.

"I thought this was how it worked."

"What worked?"

"How you make friends."

"That's what we're doing?"

He shrugged.

"Most of my friends don't ask me about my past love life."

"Most of your friends aren't naked in front of a room full of women when your ex crashes in."

"True."

"Look, man. I'm not prying. Just curious. It's a hell of a coincidence, isn't it? Of all the people in the world to serve you inheritance papers, it happens to be the woman you were engaged to?"

Coincidence.

The television flashed with a new story, this one about some billionaire who died and how his will was being executed. One of those names Gerald had heard a hundred times since his youth. Declan followed Gerald's gaze and laughed softly, the sound closer to a snicker.

"Dad hated that guy."

"Who?"

Declan nudged his chin toward the television. "Harold Hopewell. Billionaire. Routinely beat Dad on those stupid money magazine lists for top billionaires."

"Huh." The papers Suzanne had given him suddenly burned a hole in his back pocket as a preternatural creeping sensation took over all the bare skin on his body.

Coincidence.

Five shots later, Declan paid for all the beer, grudgingly shaking Gerald's hand after being soundly trounced. He did not reveal any details about his honeymoon. The two kicked back in uncomfortable, slightly sticky wooden chairs, and watched an anemic darts game being played by two drunk old geezers wearing Marines baseball hats.

"So this is how people hang out." Declan watched as Gerald peeled the corner of the label on his beer. "You just waste time and shoot the shit." He frowned, then sniffed. "This place smells like Louie's Last Stand."

"What's that?"

"A dive casino that Anterdec owns in Las Vegas."

"I think all old bars have a scent they patent. It's the smell of desperation, defeat, and lovesick tears."

"And anger," Declan added. He sniffed again. "And old Fritos."

"And puke."

Declan shot him a disgusted look.

"You're the hospitality industry expert."

"Not anymore. Now I'm just a coffee chain owner."

"You'll never be *just* anything, sir—er, Declan."

The two stood at the same time, as if thinking the same thought.

"Gotta go—"

"Time to head out—"

"I'll get you next time," Declan vowed, face tight at the memory of losing. "You snookered me."

"Yeah, but I'm the one who spilled his guts." Gerald laughed as the blast of outside air caught him short, his inhale a shock. This part of Boston was gentrifying, filled with a mix of old shabby bars and fried-food joints and trendy haute-cuisine bistros. Lofts were being carved out of the old warehouses above the street-level shops. It was the It Neighborhood, and the Westside Center for the Arts was both benefitting and hurting from the change.

More people than ever were coming to the classes and supporting the cause.

And the landlord was about to double their rent.

"I'm a street kid. Had to learn to shark it," he admitted.

Declan's face clouded. "An actual street kid?"

"Nah. Not homeless. But my parents were what they call 'free range.' Lots of time on my hands. Too many bars nearby. I was playing for ice cream money by twelve."

"At twelve, I was taking ballroom dancing lessons and spending summers in Russia working on the language," Declan answered.

The two looked at each other.

And shrugged.

The last two blocks to the garage near the arts center were a quick trip, the booze giving Gerald a buzz, the conversation both jarring and deeply satisfying. You spend years elevating someone to a position of authority because you have no choice, and then you get to know them for who they really are.

And find out that the very personal underbelly is even better.

Chapter Four

Suzanne really *did* have a date. She wasn't lying. Stacking the timing of events was intentional, so she could have an out.

Also, so she could feel the smug satisfaction from Gerald's reaction.

At least, that's what she thought she wanted.

Instead, she felt sick to her stomach, still reeling from the look on his face.

The dinner date was at a restaurant just four blocks away, so she walked, her feet killing her from wearing high heels all day, but sore arches were the least of her worries. My God. Gerald.

How could a man look better after ten years?

He'd never been a classically handsome man. When they'd first met in Afghanistan, he looked like any other angry soldier. Second tour of duty, worn down and worn in, Gerald had gleaming blue eyes that changed color with whatever he wore, shaved his tawny hair to bald perfection, and wore government-issue uniforms like they were cut to fit him for a *Men's Health* cover shot. He had a body like a personal trainer combined with a Navy SEAL.

Which was—to a T—Gerald.

Suzanne had gotten off the transport plane and run into him, tripping on the final step of the ramp, her bag in hand flying in an arc.

The guy had caught it—one-handed—by the handles, his other hand on her elbow, steadying her.

And he hadn't moved a step.

"Careful." That word. That voice. Like an old-fashioned disk jockey from the 1960s, all funk and sex appeal in vocal cord form, but with a military edge.

This was a man in command of himself.

She wanted to lose control in that voice.

Their eyes locked, and the brush of his fingertips against hers as he handed her the bag had said more than any response she could give, her addled mind, her racing heart capable only of an anemic, "Thank you."

He'd looked at her and paused, clearly hiding emotion. "Ensign Dayton."

They were equals.

She returned the favor.

"Ensign Wright."

Now she faced a different introduction, one under considerably more stress, but in an environment that was about forty degrees cooler.

Like her heart.

Life in the States, especially in big cities like Boston, still caught her off-guard at odd moments. Two years she'd spent in Afghanistan, and thirty-two years she'd spent living in the U.S., and yet it was the sophisticated, high-stress, high-gloss life of modern urban America that felt foreign at times.

Grizzled vets often told her that life back home was too stretched out, like taffy (though that's not the metaphor they'd used).

"Living life back home as a civilian is all stretched out like a whore's hole after a ship come to port," was the exact quote of the other NCOs had said during a rare clandestine drinking session on a brief R&R in Kabul.

She preferred the taffy comparison.

44

* * *

She spotted her date the second she walked into the restaurant.

Normally, she had a split-second judgment that kicked in when it came to people. One of three reactions:

The Hallelujah Chorus.

A sad trombone.

Radio silence.

Radio it was, then. Her date didn't trigger any highs or lows inside, which meant this could go either way.

He was fine looking, with short middle-brown hair the color of a drab leather briefcase, stylish glasses without a frame at the bottom, and the scanning eyes of someone who knew how to work a room.

Or who thought he did.

"Suzanne?" He stood, one hand going up to the perfectly knotted red-checked tie, the move calculated. As she moved closer, she saw his eyes were a dark brown, perfectly even, as if someone took chocolate paint and spread it with precision.

She knew he was showing off his Patek Philippe watch and gold cuff links on his wrist with that move. Good for him. The items were a sign of success, an outward signal designed to convey a message.

Message received.

"Steve James?"

He grinned, holding out a smooth hand, with fingernails buffed and perfectly manicured. "That's the name I use on the dating site. My first and middle name. I'm actually Steve Raleigh," he said, looking around the room, his voice elevated. "So great to finally have the pleasure of being with you, Suzanne."

Well.

He looked at her like he expected her to know who he was. As if Steve Raleigh were a celebrity, like he'd just announced he was Brad Pitt or Matt Damon.

Over the last year, a new breed of guy had emerged in Suzanne's online dating foibles: the networking dater. He was less likely to find her on OKCupid and more likely to pick her because of her LinkedIn profile.

In other words, he wasn't looking for a passion partner, with romantic walks on the beach, candlelit dinners, and weekends spent in bed on Nantucket.

He was looking for business connections, to rub elbows instead of lips, and to find a leg up in his corporate ladder-climbing.

As a partner at one of the biggest law firms in Boston, Suzanne was a prime piece of filet mignon in this dating meat market.

That turn of phrase—*the pleasure of being with you*—was a new one for her, though.

"Excuse me, I just have to tell you something," he said suddenly, moving in front of her as if he were interrupting her. He wasn't.

She was standing perfectly still.

"I just have to tell you how fabulous your hair looks." He smiled, tilting his head, the move somehow practiced and genuine at the same time.

It threw her into a tailspin.

"Thank you." Instinct kicked in and she reached up, touching a thick wave that fell over her shoulder.

He grinned, pulled out her chair, and she sat, flummoxed.

Was this guy a networker? Trying to study him without being obvious, she watched as he adjusted his tie again, angling his wrist awkwardly to make the entire face of the watch show.

"Nice watch," she said, being polite.

"What, this?" His eyebrow arched. "Just an old family heirloom." Eyes drifting to her breasts, he made it clear he liked what he saw. "Your pendant is beautiful." He caught her gaze. "And so are you."

"Thank you." The direct approach often worked with her. He was intriguing.

"So tell me more about you," he said, eyes on her face, searching. Then he reached into his pocket, grabbed his phone, glanced at it, and put it back.

"Don't we need to order?"

He waved his hand. "Already took care of it."

She looked askance, trying to decide how she felt about that. "How do you know what I like?"

"I'll surprise you."

"Let me guess—beef." He looked like the type to order steaks because he thought they were more manly. To be fair, he also had the body of a guy following Paleo, with a tall, lean, hungry look.

"You know me so well." When he smiled, he was a handsome guy, if guarded. "You're from Oklahoma, right?" he asked abruptly.

Why the weird topic change?

"Minnesota, actually."

"You don't have an accent."

She gave him a tight smile. "Military brat. My dad was a naval officer. We moved a lot. Minnesota's where I finished high school."

"You claim it as your home state?"

"Something like that." She took a sip of water. "You from a military family, Steve? Did you serve?"

"Me? No," he scoffed.

"Why not?" She withheld judgment from her voice, even if he wasn't extending the same courtesy to her.

"Never needed to."

"Define 'need.'"

"Let's talk more about you," he insisted, saved by the introduction of a tray of cooked, chilled vegetables and dressings, the first course.

"I'm a combat veteran and a lawyer. What more do you need to know?"

"I'm sure you're more than that."

"I don't need to be more than that."

"You're a woman, too."

Never said I wasn't, she thought, but didn't say.

"You're a full partner. Did it in seven years. And with a non-top-ten law degree," he said, adding a sniff that was meant to express praise.

Bzzz.

His phone. He pulled it out, glanced at her, then laughed. With an open and friendly manner, he moved his chair closer to hers and reached out, grazing his fingers against her shoulder. "Check this out."

As she studied the pictures on his phone, she watched him flip through picture after picture of local celebrities, high-ranking business people, and an array of high-status women in twos and threes. This was his Twitter stream.

"@bigdealmkr?"

"Right." He smirked, took the phone back, and looked at her. "You know who Jessica Coffin is, right?"

What a strange *non sequitur*. "Sure. Who lives in Boston and doesn't know who she is?"

"We're good friends." He announced this with a studied casual tone.

"You have many good friends in Boston society, it seems." She nodded toward his phone, which he was currently using. "Looks like you're well connected."

He puffed up. Inadvertently, she'd said exactly what he wanted to hear. "It's just how my life is. You know." He flipped from one app to another and flashed a picture of James McCormick, Steve, and two attractive young women at a charity ball from three months ago.

"Partying with the McCormicks?"

"And those two models. One of them was made swimsuit model of the year." His eyes jumped from the screen to her, as if keeping track of something.

"Nice."

God, this was boring.

The waiter appeared with a bottle of red wine, which he uncorked. Pouring a mouthful for Steve, the waiter handed the glass to her date, who made a dog and pony show over a $20 bottle of wine that Suzanne regularly drank for $10 a bottle, on sale at her local liquor store.

When he was done winning the wine Olympics, Steve nodded for the waiter to pour a full glass.

Suzanne covered hers, looked at the waiter with a dazzling smile, and said, "I would prefer a nice glass of Riesling." She only had so many carbs she could eat per day, and all of them would be wine at the rate this date was going.

The outraged look on his face seemed so out of proportion to her request.

This guy was blowing hot and cold. Perplexed, Suzanne tried to figure him out. Part of her liked him— the compliments certainly were nice.

"But this is an Argentine steakhouse. We'll have beef."

"What's wrong with white wine and beef?"

His eyes flew open, the gleam of triumph abundantly clear. He was about to *school* her.

The creeping sensation that this whole interaction was rolling out with an unspoken subtext rolled over her like a gust of wind that starts as a breeze and turns into a gale-force blast. He was playing a game she didn't even know existed, operating by social rules she didn't know.

She'd never, ever had a date like this.

The waiter delivered her wine. Steve crinkled his nose in disgust as she took a sip.

"That blouse would flatter you more if it were paired with something that emphasized your waist and helped to hide your hips," he said in a sudden, stiff tone.

"Excuse me?" Where was *this* coming from?

"It looks nice, of course." He sipped his water. "But it could look so much better if you put some effort into it."

And that was it. The words didn't matter. The attitude did. In those two sentences, Steve Raleigh conveyed contempt in ways she'd felt and experienced before.

And would not tolerate.

She wanted to rip his nose off and shove it up his ass.

Instead, she leaned forward seductively, the top of her blouse opening up, exposing the tips of her black lace bra. He looked down. She'd have been surprised if he hadn't. Circling the top of her wine glass with a manicured middle finger, she opened her mouth, licked her lips, and said:

"We're wasting our time here, aren't we?" she said.

One corner of his mouth quirked up, his own sultry smile matching hers. He didn't get the double meaning, hearing only what he wanted to hear.

The server, a woman, was in the middle of pouring more red wine for Steve when the neck of the bottle clattered against the rim of his glass, making a teeth-rattling sound, spilling a few drops of wine on the tablecloth.

"Do you mind? We're dining here," he snapped. "You need to be better about how you pour," he chided. "No wonder it's so hard to find good help these days. People are sloppy."

50

The server said nothing, jaw clenching. Her eyes met Suzanne's and she held her gaze. "Sorry."

Yeah. Me too, lady. Me, too.

"Hmph," Steve replied.

"What do you do for a living, Steve?" Suzanne asked. If she was stuck with him for another half hour, might as well make small talk.

Behind his glasses, wary, calculating eyes narrowed. "You didn't Google me?"

"No."

He laughed, a genuine sound that made her soften slightly. "Googling a date is so commonplace now, I assumed you'd done it. Don't pretend you didn't. You know who I am. I'm an investment banker." He named the top firm in the city. "And I know what you do, obviously. You've done well at Phelps, Miller. Then again, plenty of lawyers can do well in small ponds like that firm."

It hit her.

She suddenly knew exactly what he was doing. He glanced at his phone again and she realized:

He'd been negging her.

"Excuse me," she said, standing. Steve was clearly well mannered, for he stood respectfully as she walked away to the ladies' room, struggling to keep her shoulders relaxed, her purse clutched in her fist. As she turned the corner she saw his head bent over the blue glow of his phone screen.

Great.

Her hands flushed hot and cold as she reached into her purse, resting on the settee as she texted her best friend, Kari.

RESCUE TEXT NEEDED! she typed.

Ten seconds later, her best friend replied.

Damn! Sorry. Will text. That bad?

Hard to explain, but it's bad.

51

Need me to come in person and pretend to be your lover?

Kari had done that once. It blew up in their faces when the date asked for a threesome.

Never mind, Kari wrote, as if reading her mind. *Didn't go so well last time.*

I draw the line at tongue kissing you, Suzanne tapped, laughing to herself. *Bad enough we shared a sleeping bag that one time when we camped in Montana.*

I'm only a lesbian when it's negative two degrees outside, Kari joked. *What's he doing?*

Negging me! Only it's like he's following a script, she replied.

Her phone rang.

"Suz, *is* he following a script? Remember that dating service I mystery shopped, where we were trained on anti-PUA techniques?"

Kari pronounced the word like *POO-uh*.

"Poo-uh?"

"Pick-up artist."

"Oh, God. Is that what he's doing? Why? Why do guys do this shit?"

"Did he start out with something like, 'I just have to tell you—' and then flatter you?"

Suzanne's stomach went cold. "Yes."

"And did he show you pictures of himself surrounded by hot women and elite men?"

"Oh my God, Kari, yes!" Her voice went high and screechy. "How did you know?"

"And now he's negging you."

"Yes!"

"He's following the Eight Tips."

"What are 'the Eight Tips'?"

"These PUA trainers have workshops and books where they train guys on how to get women to sleep

52

with them. There's a famous list of eight tips for bagging a woman."

"*Bagging?* I'm about as likely to sleep with Steve Raleigh as I am to shove a breadstick up my ass."

"Thanks for the visual. You know I'm eating dinner right now." Kari paused. "Steve Raleigh, huh? I'll Google him for you when we're off the phone."

"Sorry. What do I do?" she asked. Kari was more worldly when it came to dating. "I just want to tell him off and disappear."

"You could," Kari mused. "But what about having some fun with him?"

"Fun? You call this fun?"

"What if you turn it around on him? Make him suffer a little."

"Now you're talking my language. How?"

"If he's really following a script, then his next step is kee-no."

"KEE-no? Like the game?"

"No. K-I-N-O. It's this stupid phrase that's short for kinesthetics. He's going to start covertly touching you in non-sexual places as a test to see where your physical boundaries are."

"You mean he'll groom me."

"Basically."

"This is so gross."

"Welcome to the world of the pick-up artist. You're an object. An animal who can be trained."

"So turn the training right back around on him?"

"Exactly. He won't know what hit him."

"So what do I do?"

"KINO is all about quietly touching you. They start with the shoulder. The knee. The arm. Then they move on to brush the side-boob, the hip, and so forth. They're testing your bounds."

"So I give it back?"

"But on your terms, Suz." Kari started giggling.

Aha. Suzanne was starting to understand.

"What else? What's next?"

"Sexual dialing."

"Like a booty call?"

"No, no. He'll just dial it up. Start touching you on the belly, the breast, and so forth. Making it clear he wants sex."

"Eww."

"You know how cross-examination works in a courtroom, right?"

"What does that have to do with my awkward date?"

"Think about it, Suz. Use his techniques against him."

Epiphany. Lightbulb.

"Got it."

"Next, he'll argue with you about some stupid thing."

"He's already done that. Who cares if I drink white wine with beef? He got really weird about that one."

"It's called 'qualification.' They do it to be all alpha and prove they're not boring. He'll do it again."

"Too late."

"And the final move is to get you into bed or get your number, but he'll do it in a way that makes you think he's rejecting you."

"He already has my number."

"Then he's going for the pink hole."

"Kari!"

"Well...he is."

"KINO, dialing, qualification, pick-up." Suzanne memorized it like she was studying for the bar.

"You'll do fine. I kind of pity the guy."

"I hate this."

"I'm so sorry."

Suzanne just sighed.

Kari began to giggle. "Suz? How much makeup do you have in your purse?"

"Makeup? I'm not wasting one more second on looking nice for that loser!"

"No, no. I have an idea. Shake out all your makeup."

Thirty seconds later, Suzanne stared at two lipsticks, a mascara tube, some rouge, and a metallic-blue eyeliner left over from the last time she saw her teen niece.

She recited the items to Kari.

"Unbutton the top two buttons of your blouse."

"My nipples will show!"

"That's the point."

"What?"

"Can you picture an online mail order bride? The kind on those dating sites where—"

"The kind that men who use PUA techniques frequent?"

"Exactly. Whore yourself up. With makeup, I mean. Go for it. Go overboard. He wants a hot woman? Give him one. Scare him off."

Suzanne looked at her phone with an increasingly dubious expression. "You're not punking me, are you?"

"I swear. Trust me."

She picked up the mascara wand and applied three coats, until her eyelashes tangled in her eyebrow hairs. "Mascara done."

"Now run the mascara wand through your eyebrows."

"WHAT?"

"Really go for it. Trust me. He's going to be the one on edge when you walk back out, all confident and done to the nines."

"I'll be done to the ninety-nines if I mascara-tint my eyebrows."

"You know those Facetuning apps we make fun of? When people from our high schools use the makeup apps on their selfies and think no one will notice that their nose now looks like an eraser crashed into it and their eyes have the glow of an Avatar character?"

"Yeah."

"You're aiming for a real-life version of that, Suzanne."

Two minutes later and she stared at a grotesque version of herself, hair pulled up in a rough updo, eyes like raccoon claws, eyebrows darker than Elvira's, and lipstick so red she might as well join the pageant circuit.

"I look like a woman Donald Trump would date."

"SUCCESS!" Kari shouted. "Take a picture and text me."

Suzanne did.

Ten seconds later, she heard a low whistle from Kari. "Oh, Suzanne. You're...breathtaking."

"Yeah. I can't breathe when I look in the mirror, either. Kari, what if a client comes here and sees me like this?"

"When did you start caring what your clients think?"

Good point.

"Open your shirt more. Show a little lace."

Suzanne did.

"And add one more layer of lipstick."

"I'll need paint thinner to take it off if I do that."

"Yes."

Suzanne complied.

"You did it. Now go out there like you're on the prowl. And use all the PUA techniques against him."

Suzanne ended the call, shoved her phone in her purse, used the facilities, and went back to the table with a heavy heart.

Even if she was hardened and cynical, even if she knew Steve was using her for business information, it didn't take away the sting.

Every date was a balloon filled with hope. Sometimes the balloon was filled with helium.

This time, it was full of shit.

And when it popped...

Squaring her shoulders, she looked for the table, her vision now obscured by so much mascara that everything in the restaurant looked like the woods from *The Blair Witch Project*.

As she bent her knees to sit, Steve said, "Cue your rescue text in five, four, three, two,—"

Bzzz.

He smirked, clearly expecting her to be embarrassed, pleased with himself for the barb.

She shrugged. "Can I help it if my friend has a bad case of premature emasculation?"

Steve paled.

She looked at the phone.

Check his Twitter stream, Suz. That guy's a total ass.

Steve did a double take across the table and peered at her, cataloguing her face, examining her neck and breasts with a wolfish intensity as she tapped her Twitter app, remembered his handle, and—there it was.

A stream of real time texts over the last twenty minutes.

She's about a five. Could be a seven if she tried harder.

White wine with beef? Amateur.

She served in the military. I spent six years at Boy Scout camp all summer and learned more about discipline than she seems to know. Maybe I'll have to discipline *her*.

The tweets were all aimed at a handle called PUAsucksess, but good old Steve had forgotten to put a dot in front of them, therefore making them public. It was clear from his behavior that he thought those tweets were private.

She looked up, a slow burn, to find him grinning at her.

And then it happened. Kari totally called it.

The hand.

The hand reached out and tapped her knee, an exploratory touch.

You might say he was feeling her out.

Literally.

KINO, huh?

She reached across and gently poked his ear.

His grin faltered but he scooted his chair closer, eyes on her white wine.

Tinny laughter preceded his bountiful condescension. "Didn't you learn about wine? I thought it was a prerequisite in law school." Touch.

"No. I studied *law* in law school." Poke. She poked his shoulder twice. He startled, eyebrows knitting together in confusion.

"Surely you know that moving in certain business circles is all about cultivating the right taste," he said. His palm went to her knee, staying there.

Oh, God. This was worse than that blind date with the guy who kissed his ferret on the lips.

"No." She cut him off, fast. "Moving in certain business circles is about being good at business," she replied, her hand going to his chest, palm over his heart.

His eyebrows shot up, eyes widening.

She grinned.

"But taste is taste," he said, ignoring the comment, looking down at her hand and licking his lips. "It is cultivated and rarified, and white wine and red meat together is like—"

58

"A fish riding a bicycle." She began randomly pushing on his chest, pecs, shoulders, neck and earlobe, like he was a human version of a sheet of bubble wrap.

Pop.

Pop pop pop.

"Exactly." He said the word like one praises a small child who has acquiesced, except his voice trailed off. "Drinking white wine with beef is a sign that you're, well—"

"Uncouth?" Suzanne finished off her glass.

His nose wrinkled. "Uneducated." He slid the hand on her knee up her thigh, his other hand reaching for her stomach.

Sexual dialing.

Kari wasn't just right.

She was a psychic.

"Don't worry. I'll teach you," he crooned.

"Teach me?" Her eyes widened. Oh, brother. Deciding to play along, she pretended to be appreciative. "That would be great, Steve. I am already learning so much from you."

Like the fact that she'd rather date a guy who kisses his ferrets.

This was the problem with having Gerald as an ex.

Ten years.

Ten damn long years, and no one else had ever measured up.

Not that Steve Raleigh was even close.

"Hee *hee*!" she said, poking him in the stomach like he was the Pillsbury Doughboy. Twisting slightly, she broke the contact between his palm and her thigh.

"What are you doing?" he grunted, affronted by her finger poking.

"This!" She poked him again. "Just being friendly!"

His eyes narrowed, but he reached for her abdomen, clearly undaunted.

She dropped her napkin in his lap, "accidentally" overreaching for it, her half-closed hand colliding with his crotch with more force than he expected.

"Ow!"

"Sorry. I guess I'm not good at being friendly."

He let a small glare come through, then recovered, leaning in, trying yet again. "You're captivating in a way that—"

She bopped him on the nose, then pretended to "steal" it, her thumb poking out between her index and middle fingers. "Got your nose!"

Bop.

"Gave it back."

He looked at her like she was crazy.

Progress.

Then barely masked anger. Strategically, if he was dating to manipulate his way into bigger and better deals on the business circuit, he had to be nice to her. Had to take whatever she dished out.

"I would love to see how we can mutually teach each other," he said, drinking his wine.

"What do you have to offer?" She sat up slightly, eyes drifting down his body, ostentatiously stopping at his lap.

"You're...bold." The facade was beginning to crack.

"I'm me." She shrugged, taking a bite of hearts of palm, the cold slide of chilled vegetable highlighting how bizarre the past hour had been. From seeing her ex to seeing his opposite.

"Does it work?" he asked, sitting back and pulling on his tie and cuff links.

"Does what work?"

"The aggressive feminist act."

Okay. Gloves off.

"Shall we get to the point, then?" she said, shoving a piece of chilled marinated carrot in her mouth. Might as well get something in her poor stomach.

"The point?"

"You're not here to get in my pants, Steve. You're here to get into my client portfolio."

Most unctuous men would have spluttered and denied, gone out of their way to protest that they would never do such a thing.

Not Steve Raleigh.

One corner of his mouth curled up. His eyes shifted, darting around the room, assessing the layout.

And then he leaned forward, eyes on her breasts, and whispered, "You're not really my type, Suzanne. But I would love to be friends?"

The Qualification. The negative close. Wow. He was a paint-by-numbers guy.

Suzanne had to give him credit. He exhibited more male prowess than she expected. The guy was a typical frat boy, the follower, the clinger who did whatever he was told for the sake of pack mentality. She knew the type well.

She'd commanded hundreds of guys like Steve.

And she knew that she'd be in charge in the bedroom, too.

Not that it would ever get to that point.

"You're here to network. Not to screw me. Admit it."

"I'm here for the same reason you're here, Suzanne."

"Which reason is that, Steve?" she asked as he helped himself to a big chunk of red meat.

"Don't be coy."

Coy was a word that no one had *ever* applied to her.

"Coy?"

61

"You looked me up. It's cute of you to say you didn't, but you did."

"I didn't."

He smirked. "Whatever. You know that my bank and your firm have enormous potential with the MacAlister account."

Here it came.

"MacAlister." She knew the account well. It was her baby.

"I know the heirs to the company are in a vicious fight. We're invested—deep."

We, she assumed, meant Steve. Not his firm. She knew how investment bankers worked.

"And you're looking for insider information?"

He had the decency to pretend to be shocked.

"What? No. Of course not. I would never, ever violate the law." His voice was steady as a level. Was he purring? "Just two colleagues getting to know each other better, chatting about work, becoming more intimately acquainted. If we happen to discuss the MacAlister account, it's pure coincidence."

Coincidence.

She'd had quite enough coincidences for one day, thank you very much.

A part of her wished this had really been just about Steve using his PUA techniques to get in her pants. As disgusting as the synchronized, slimy gestures were, the idea that he used those techniques as a gateway to get into her business network made it all worse.

A new server appeared, a young woman with a bouncy ponytail. Shift change, apparently. "Ready for the dessert menu? Coffee? Another—"

"We're ready for the check," Suzanne and Steve said in unison.

At least they had one thing in common.

He gave her an irritated smirk. "You're hard core. Nothing like most women I date."

"What are most women you date like?"

He began to take a breath, halting midway, the puff of air artificially cut off. The sound was like someone being scared on a very cold morning.

"Not like you."

"How tautological."

"You don't need to pull out grad school words to prove your intelligence. I know what that means."

"I wouldn't have used the word if I'd thought you didn't know the meaning." She touched his hand, smiling.

He flinched. From the look on his face, he clearly didn't know whether to be flattered or offended.

"Here's the check!" Chirpy the Server announced, bouncing on the balls of her feet.

Steve picked it up, eyed Suzanne, then sat there.

Saving him the trouble, she pulled three twenties out of her purse and set them in the check folder. Her half. He matched it, remaining silent.

Without another word, they walked out of the restaurant. Expecting to separate at the covered entrance to the restaurant, Suzanne was surprised when Steve followed her up the stairs and onto the sidewalk, side by side.

"So," he said, moving closer, coming in for a kiss.

Oh, no.

No no no.

Aside from the fact that there was no way that man's tongue was getting anywhere near her, if she kissed him right now all the lipstick she wore would make him slide off onto the curb.

"Where's your car?" he asked, smiling at her in a way that made her love her dog even more.

"I took the T."

He shuddered. "How can you stand it?"

"You drive into the city every day?"

"No. I live in Back Bay now," he crowed.

"And you have a car?" That was overkill.

"Of course! A Beemer."

Of course.

She began a slow walk back toward the arts center, the ground dark with a light rain that must have fallen during their short dinner. A handful of dive bars speckled the way, mixed in with a fancy coffee shop, a bead store, a head shop, a co-working center and an ancient dry cleaner.

"Suzanne, I feel like we got off on the wrong foot," Steve announced, his voice contritely pompous. How the hell did he manage that contradiction?

"Yes?"

He reached for her elbow. She took her finger and spelled out the word 'asshole' in cursive on his chest.

He let go.

"I believe I gave you the wrong impression with this date."

She kept walking, but watched him, giving him her full attention as one does with toddlers and men wearing Jason masks.

"Yes?" she urged him. Long past the point of being romantic, the date had turned comical. At least she'd have a good story, as Kari often said after spectacularly bad dates.

"I didn't seek you out because of your partner status at your firm."

"You didn't?"

"Not initially. Your picture was gorgeous and your personal statement caught my eye."

She laughed.

"My best friend wrote that."

He perked up. "Is she single?"

64

Sliding to a halt, she was simultaneously grateful and furious when his hands reached out to steady her, her fingers gripping his forearm as one of his hands slid around her waist. Righting herself quickly, she spiraled out of his grasp.

"Can we get a selfie before you go?" Steve asked, reaching into his jacket pocket. "I have my selfie stick and we can—"

She grabbed her phone and pulled up his Twitter stream.

She came out of the bathroom looking like a goddess.
Her hand's on my crotch. Score!
Pic to follow to prove I bagged her.

Just then, the door to a bar a few feet away opened, spilling neon light and the raucous sounds of sports games and billiards into the city streets. A dark-haired man accompanied by a bald friend came into the light, then shadows, both of them tall, one bulkier and more muscular, big and rippled with—

No.

"Suzanne?"

Gerald.

"STEVE?"

Declan.

Her hands flew to her face. She looked like Pennywise the Clown married Tammy Faye Bakker.

"What a wonderful coincidence!" Steve called out, looking like a kid wandering the streets playing Pokemon Go who found a Dragonite. "Declan McCormick! How's it going, my friend?"

And then Steve grabbed Declan in a manbrace, the bromance version of a hug.

Suzanne had seen Gerald in combat, bullets whizzing by, IEDs destroying jeeps, body parts flying and hardened soldiers screaming for their mamas. She'd watched him during ten days without a shower, seen him struggle on a half hour of sleep a night for five days straight, and witnessed countless acts of stress-filled bravery.

Not once had she ever seen a look of utter shock on his face like *this*.

As she watched him, Gerald's shoulders expanded, chest growing, arms flexing in a primal move that made it clear he was preparing to defend Declan in some physical way.

"What the hell?" Declan said, shoving Steve away. "What are you doing? I hate you!"

Declan McCormick was her new favorite client.

"Suzanne! Surely you know my friend Declan McCormick? Of Anterdec? We go back a long way. He's such a joker!" Steve's shit-eating grin made it clear this was spectacle. More status-by-association. Performance. Nothing but show. Steve was using Declan as some kind of status symbol, as if being seen with him bolstered Steve in her eyes.

Declan looked like he was about to deck Steve.

Then again, Steve didn't seem to care what she thought. He only cared that the ruse of being friends with Declan happened at all.

"Declan," she said smoothly, reaching for the man, having met him across the boardroom table once a year for his mother's family trust. At most, she'd shaken his hand those seven times. But with a steely look that asked for his buy-in, she reached up—not much, for she was a tall woman—and planted a soft kiss on his cheek. His arms wrapped around her in a polite hug.

Her eyes met Gerald's.

Who looked like he needed to kill both men now.

She pulled away, the smug look on Steve's face making the decision for her. The next words out of her mouth had to happen.

Had to.

"Last time I saw you, Declan, you were naked."

Steve gaped.

Declan played along by grinning, arching one dark eyebrow, and making a sexy sound in the back of his throat.

Voice infused with mirth and a low, sexy innuendo, she winked at him, then looked at Steve. "By the way, Steve—your Twitter stream is public." She looked down at herself, then looked back up, and poked him in the belly. "And I am *so* not a 5."

And without another word, she walked away, using the old runway model's gait Kari taught her in college, knowing three sets of eyes were on her backside.

She only cared about one of them.

And he was the only guy she hadn't just touched.

CHAPTER FIVE

"What just happened?" Steve said, his voice like a hot snot bubble. "I don't understand. Naked? Suzanne's seen you naked?" He looked at Declan, pointing an accusing finger. "Are you on a mission to sleep with every woman I've ever dated?"

"Shut up. And don't you ever touch me again," Declan snapped, making Gerald turn to Steve, blood pumping, his eyes taking in his opponent.

"But—"

"And you think she's a 5? You tweeted that? Are you *crazy*?" Declan shouted.

"Hey, man, she didn't have all that hot makeup on and that low-cut shirt at first. Now she's a 7, maybe a—"

"Shut up!" Declan and Gerald said together.

"She's at least an 8," Declan argued. "And one thousand times out of your league."

"What were *you* doing with her?" Gerald demanded of Steve in a low predator's voice, not giving a shit what anyone thought, though the fact that Declan and Steve were talking about Suzanne as a number was getting old. Fast.

"I was on a date!"

"You were her date? *You?*" Gerald felt the animal in him flaring up, the deep, feral part of him that made rational thought splinter into thousands of slivers of himself. If he let it get the better of him, he'd lose days. Possibly a week. No way could this wasteoid fleshbag of festering ball sacs named Steve Raleigh unleash the phantom inside him that took over.

No.

Absolutely not.

Declan whipped around and looked at Gerald, eyes narrowing, sensing danger.

"Get the fuck out of here," Declan said to Steve, who didn't need to be told twice, skittering away like a frightened spider.

The sound of Declan breathing hard through his nose, body tensed and ready for fight, was all Gerald heard, until Declan muttered, "What did Shannon ever see in that douchebag?"

Gerald worked on his breathing, vision turning to fire at the edges, the rush of adrenaline and the sparks in his brain zapping him into nothingness. Suzanne was on a date with that slimeball? He knew exactly who Steve Raleigh was, under specific orders when Shannon and Declan started dating that Steve was considered to be a borderline stalker.

And an unctuous twat.

Declan's exact words.

The thought of that bastard's hands on Suzanne made Gerald's own hands shake in rage, his thighs tightening, knees unlocking, ready to pounce. Red rage poured through him like water at a baptism, hellfire and brimstone turning his prior calm into a distant memory.

"Hey. Hey," Declan said, his voice firmer. "You look like you're about to pop a vein."

"I'm about to pop *him*."

"And that would land you in jail for assault. He's just the type to sue."

"Dead men can't sue."

"And jailed chauffeurs can't teach great art classes."

Gerald knew Declan was methodically talking him down, and simultaneously unnerved by the situation. Years of carefully controlling his emotions under tightly

70

calibrated work conditions meant that Declan had only seen the placid, stoic version he showed the world.

Not *this* self.

And this had been the side of him that had dominated ten years ago, when he'd broken up with Suzanne for her own good.

A flash of movement under a streetlight in the distance, at the nearest light, caught Gerald's eye.

Suzanne.

Sprinting, he left Declan befuddled, calling out his name, until the light changed and he watched as Suzanne marched forward with that confident walk of hers, shoulders squared as if she were still in morning formation and wore a uniform, wiping her mouth with a tissue and muttering to herself. He knew how the curve of her spine felt under his palms when she stood like that, the supple feel of the paradox between soft skin and hard bone a delightful feast for his fingers.

"Wait!" he called out, unsure and unbidden, moving on pure instinct. He needed to touch her. Would die without making that single, simple connection. Not just in an intimate sense. The need was more than that.

Suzanne got to the curb and stopped. She did not turn around, her body poised, waiting.

Panting with the burst of exertion, his brain firing on all cylinders, he caught up to her and slowed down at the last steps, moving to her, pulled by a force that drew him in. His front settled against her back, his tight cotton t-shirt brushing against the thin linen jacket she wore, the friction erotic and full, sensual.

As his palms touched her elbows, her arms at her side, he inhaled with precision, measuring her.

She did not move.

"Suzanne," he murmured, chin close to a stray hair that curled out from her updo, resting against the fine, creamy line of her neck. With longer hair, the sharp, jutting bones of her jaw stood out, giving her the look of a Viking princess. In heels, she was exactly his height, setting him off-kilter. He wasn't a short man. In fatigues she was always four to five inches shorter. In service dress, her shoes gave her a two-inch lift.

He liked being equal. Liked it a lot.

"Please," she whispered, the word spiraling off into the dark night, as if the street lights beyond them were pulling her voice to them.

Taking her reaction as something other than rejection, he left his hands where they were, closing the inch gap between them. She was cool and regal, his hot, thick chest pressing into her back.

"Please what?" he asked, knowing this could go either way, but not caring, because right now—as each second ticked by—he had more internal calm than he'd had in ten years.

Even as desire burned bright inside him.

"Please don't."

He froze.

"Don't what?" Tempted to step back, he held strong. Her *please* carried a weight to it, a meaning he needed to discern before acting. All impulse and no analysis would end this in a flash. Time was his friend. Patience.

Hesitation.

He had to go against instinct.

"Don't start something you don't intend to finish."

Letting go of her arms, he circled her, facing the woman he'd loved so fiercely ten years ago that he'd let her go, to protect her.

From him.

Time had been so good to her, crazy makeup excepted. He reached up, half her face in shadow, the other half lit by a nearby streetlight, the effect like a Picasso painting, a Dalí, a surreal melding of the past and present, of good and evil, of yearning and rejection.

Their lips touched before he could think, restraint gone, impulse taking over and driving his body to hers, the ache of self-sacrifice finally—finally—too much to bear alone. She stepped into him, entering his orbit, and when her hands cupped his hips, pulling him close, he groaned, the sound a sigh ten years in the making.

For years, he'd shut himself off from questioning his decision. Compartmentalizing was how he survived, and Suzanne went into a little metal lockbox, a locker full of every memory, a place isolated into submission.

As she kissed him again, her mouth open, lips taking him in, his tongue finding solace and sweetness as it stroked hers, years washed away. What if that welded-shut box of emotion could be opened? What if it wasn't Pandora's box, but instead long-buried treasure?

Her kiss told him nothing.

And everything.

Roving fingers traced the lines of his shoulder blades, her palms riding up to cup the back of his neck. She made a sound of despair mixed with pleasure, which perfectly described his current state. She tasted so good. So real.

So forbidden.

And then she broke the kiss, stepping out of his arms, those same hands that had just played with his contours held palms out.

"Stop. *Stop.*" Was she talking to him, or herself?

"I stopped." Didn't want to, but he did.

"What is this, Gerald? You can't just chase me down and kiss me like that."

"You want me to kiss you a different way? Because that can be arranged." He ran a thumb along her jawline, deeply amused and perplexed by the strange makeup.

"I want an explanation."

"You want an explanation? You're the one who interrupted my class and then went on a date with my ex-boss's wife's ex-boyfriend."

"I need a Venn diagram to deconstruct that sentence, Gerald."

"How about I draw you a flow chart after a drink?"

Her speculative glare gave him hope. She wasn't saying *no*.

"Why now?"

"Because you found me."

"Found you? I've known where you are for years. I didn't find you. I was forced to encounter you."

"Forced?"

"Yes," she said with a vicious bitterness that came out as a hiss. "I'm not in the habit of tracking down men who propose to me and then walk away without explanation."

"I would hope not. That would be a terrible hobby."

She didn't laugh.

"You don't get to do this," she said slowly, tumblers in her mind clicking with Swiss precision he could feel in his bones. "You can't waltz back in my life, kiss me, and joke with me. Not after what you did."

I was afraid I'd do even worse.

The thought slammed through him like a word weapon, cutting to the quick, slicing through layers of scar tissue built around his soul.

"Walking away was wrong," he admitted. Ten years. He'd had ten years to prepare for this moment, to know what to say, except he'd never envisioned this. Not once. He'd assumed he would never see her again. That it was for the best.

Or so he'd assumed.

"Wrong? *Wrong?* You use these words, Gerald, like they have meaning. Do you have any idea how pathetic *wrong* sounds? How about walking away like that was *inhumane*? How about *soul-crushing*? How about—"

She jerked as if electrocuted, her breath a jagged series of gasps, her anger a shockwave that caught him in its path. As if gravity weighed it down, the clip in her hair dislodged, dragging the thick abundance of her blonde waves down, giving her a Greek goddess look, one curl spilling over a shoulder, the rest of her hair full around her face, eyes standing out, painted to stand out.

"No. I won't do this. Just no. You have your papers, you can process the inheritance, and I'm done. I'll assign a junior associate whether my boss likes it or not." She turned to leave.

In a fit of desperation he grabbed her, the kiss unreal, less about passion and more about the unrelenting fear that he'd never, ever see her again if he didn't try. She went with it, kissing him back with a violence that made his mouth fill with copper, the taste of her wrath the penance he had to pay. Their mouths slanted, lips softened, the kiss less a surprise and now a pleading, one they felt their way through.

"God, I've missed you," he confessed, then let her go, walking away, giving her the space she wanted.

Because to stay would have been wrong, too.

CHAPTER SIX

"Let me tell you about my crazy day," Suzanne's friend Kari announced as they settled on Suzanne's couch in sweats, munching their way through a bag of chips. Blonde like Suzanne, Kari had honey-brown eyes with thick, short lashes and a permanently curious expression on her face.

Smoochy, Suzanne's bichon frise, wriggled a spot between them, staring at her with begging eyes.

"Sorry, Smoochy," Kari said with great affect. "Your mommy won't let me give you a potato chip."

Getting a dog had been Suzanne's latest move in her ongoing attempt to pretend to have a real life. Smoochy was a rescue, a seven-year-old whose owner had been moved into a nursing home down in Florida about eight months ago. Once a month, Suzanne dutifully sent printed pictures of Smoochy to Elizabeth, her old owner, who was slipping further into Alzheimer's. But then once a month, so far, Smoochy received a letter from Elizabeth, which Suzanne read aloud to the dog.

Smoochy blinked and looked at Kari, giving her a tiny plea. The whining sound was so cute that Kari relented. Smoochy munched on the tiny piece like it was a feast.

"Your crazy day? Pfft. Bet mine beats yours." Suzanne shoved her paw into the chip bag and halted. Potato chips and her low carb diet didn't mix, damn it. Reluctantly, she left snack nirvana to Kari and walked to the kitchen, rummaging in the fridge.

"Did you have to pretend to have IBS so you could schedule a colonoscopy and inspect the cleanliness of a probe while avoiding being caught?" Kari asked pointedly. Smoochy shivered suddenly, her whole body doing a shimmy, as if she were emotionally reacting to Kari's words.

"I would trade doing that for what I actually went through." An anal probe vs. Steve Raleigh? No contest.

"That was a crazy date. I give you credit. But an asshole versus a guy who looks at assholes all day for a living? C'mon."

"I saw Gerald for the first time in ten years," Suzanne said, as if holding her place in the lineup of horrors to be shared.

Kari and Suzanne had met back in college, at freshman orientation, when Kari was a student and Suzanne the instructor. They'd been fast friends since, though their paths had diverged radically. Suzanne's ROTC scholarship led her off to war the week after she'd graduated at twenty-one, while Kari had gone into fashion design, then merchandising, and finally mystery shopping management. She managed a big division for Fokused Shop-rite, one of the biggest mystery shopping and consumer optimization companies in the country.

Right now, though, she was using her breasts to catch broken potato chips, so...

"No way! Way to bury the lede, Suzanne. What happened?"

"I saw Declan McCormick naked, served Gerald with inheritance paperwork that might be worth nine figures, and went on a date with a blowhard who makes Donald Trump look like Mother Teresa."

Kari stared at her, mouth open, like Dory the fish.

Smoochy walked out of the room, curled into a ball in her dog bed, and covered her eyes with her paws.

"I know. It's a lot," Suzanne said with a laugh, grabbing her bag of carrot sticks, dipping them in sour cream and crunching away.

"You saw Declan McCormick naked?" Kari gasped. "Is he as hot in the flesh as he is in a suit?"

Suzanne's cheeks went pink. The taste of Gerald, the brush of his lips, the sweep of his tongue in her mouth and those hands, oh those hands on her back, so masterful and yearning, had completely driven the vision of Declan McCormick's nude body out of her mind.

Okay. *Mostly* driven the vision of Declan McCormick's nude body out of her mind.

There might be a tiny remnant of memory remaining.

Or *not so* tiny.

"Suz!" Kari whapped her arm. "Get out of your drool! Spill! Share details!"

"About Gerald's kiss?"

Kari inhaled sharply, hands on her chest, her palms beginning to flap in overeager excitement. "He kissed you! Was this while Declan McCormick was naked?" Her eyes flew wide open. "Was this a threesome? Omigod, you had a threesome with Declan Mc—wait. He's married. I know Shannon. We've worked together on an account. She's going to be devastated!" Kari alternated between glaring at Suzanne as if she'd *actually* had a threesome with Declan McCormick, and processing her disappointment if Suzanne *hadn't*.

"I did not have a threesome with Declan and Gerald."

Kari's face fell. Disappointment won.

"Well, at least I don't have to be the bearer of bad news for Shannon," Kari muttered, staring at the carrot in Suzanne's hand. "And yum! When did you start eating that combination?"

"Desperation. This no-sugar, no-grains diet is making me try damn near anything."

"Combined with your lack of sex, your desperation meter is about as high as can be."

Suzanne pulled out her fiercest naval recruit stare.

"That—that doesn't work—on me. Oh, damn." Kari shielded her eyes. "You could play Nurse Ratched if they ever do a remake of *One Flew Over the Cuckoo's Nest*."

Suzanne snorted. "She was an amateur."

"Or Dolores Umbridge."

Better.

"He broke your heart all those years ago." Kari gave her a sympathetic side-eye. "You finally stopped talking about him a few years ago."

"I know." Suzanne shut herself up with a carrot.

"And stopped going to therapy."

Smoochy made an adorable snoring sound from her little bed.

"Right," she sighed, the food turning tasteless.

"Are you okay?"

"No," Suzanne answered honestly. "He kissed me. Twice. But no explanation. No offer to talk. Just kissing."

"That's more action than you've gotten in a while."

Suzanne opened her mouth to protest, then shut it. Kari wasn't wrong.

Letting out a shaky sigh, she closed her eyes. "Seeing him was brutal." Her throat tightened. Suzanne wasn't a crier. When she got emotional, she became angry.

Sadness washed over her, making her hungry.

"Want to go on an ice cream run?" She asked Kari on impulse.

Kari's eyebrow arched. "Run? As in, running? Because the last time you broke your low carb diet, you ran three miles to justify the sugar. Last time I ran three miles was, um, never. Does *never* work?"

Suzanne gave her a pitying pout. "C'mon! I'll run, you Uber. Let's go out for a big, fat sundae."

"Only if you promise to tell me exactly what happened tonight. And listen to how I got asked for my phone number by a hot proctologist."

"Kari, 'hot' and 'proctologist' don't go together."

"Neither do running and ice cream." Kari gave her a hard stare.

Laughing, Suzanne went to her bedroom, quickly threw on running clothes, and began stretching at the front door. "Toscanini's?" Suzanne lived in Charlestown. The Cambridge ice cream-slash-coffee shop was exactly 2.9 miles away. Yes, she'd clocked it.

More than a few times.

"Fine. I think you're insane, but I'm not turning down ice cream and your story."

"If you won't turn down a proctologist, why would you turn down anything?"

"Hey. If you had seen this guy..." Kari began fanning herself.

"He looks up people's buttholes for a living."

Kari shrugged. "I don't judge." She got a dreamy look on her face. "Maybe he knows his way around that part of the body better than—"

"STOP!" Suzanne gently led Smoochy to her little crate. The dog was so obedient. So passive. Suzanne had never heard her bark. Not once. She settled into her bed and resumed her nap, chin on paws.

With an evil laugh, Kari tapped on her phone screen, clearly requesting an Uber as Suzanne ran out into the dark night, needing to pound away the racing thoughts about Gerald.

Please, he'd begged at the arts center.

Please what?

The words became a chant inside her as she ran, *please what please what please what* taking over until

81

she was nothing but feet, knees, hips, arms, lungs, a body in motion staying in motion, running to make the mind less important than tendon and bone. If she could just get her emotions to step back, step down, and let her body assume center stage, then the temporary relief of setting down the burden of the past might give her a break.

Pushing herself, she found a comfortable six-minute-mile pace, and in under eighteen minutes was done, panting and covered in sweat, but ready to feast.

Kari was inside, flirting with a bearded counter guy with a man bun, her spoon already deep into a sundae.

This man bun fashion had to end soon, right?

Right?

"Hey! Here's my crazy friend I was telling you about," Kari said to Man Bun, who looked at her with a grin. Bright green eyes, thick brown beard. He was what —twenty?

Why did all the guys in Cambridge look like fetuses?

On second look, she realized what appeared to be a man bun from outside was actually a nest of snakes.

The guy had long dreads curled up into a festering pile of hair.

Give Suzanne a freshly shaved recruit any day of the week.

"Hi. Salted caramel and pumpkin two scoops in a cup with hot fudge," she ordered.

The guy snapped back and saluted. "Yes, ma'am!"

Kari snickered.

Suzanne frowned.

"What was that about?"

"You pulled out your commanding tone, Suzanne. You sounded like a drill sergeant."

"No, I didn't! I just asked for ice cream."

"You have no idea how you come across sometimes. Especially when you're pissed."

82

"I am not pissed! I just want some damn ice cream!" The glare she shot Kari should have melted the store's inventory.

"Right. Totally not pissed," Kari murmured, rolling her eyes. She flashed a sweet grin at Snake Head, who winked at her.

"He's too young for you," Suzanne said in a judgy tone. She owned it.

"Is not!"

"He only wants to date you so you can smuggle him into R-rated movies."

"Suzanne!"

"And buy him cigarettes."

"He's twenty-four!"

"Which is ten years younger than you."

"Rawr." Kari pretended to be a cougar. "Young guys are impressionable. Experimental. Adventurous in bed."

"Is that all a euphemism for inexperienced? No, thanks. I don't want to have to play the sexual version of Pokemon Go with my body as a gym and my clitoris a rare Pokemon."

Kari looked at her in horror. "Way to ruin Pokemon forever! Ew! Now your clit will be in my brain forever as a Charmander." She paused, deep in thought. "But erotic Pokemon sounds like a great business idea."

The store went silent. Suzanne turned and looked around.

Everyone was staring at them.

"Uh, here's your ice cream," Snake Head said, trying to suppress a smile.

Suzanne handed him a sweat-soaked bill. Kari took the change. They skedaddled, bursting into giggles on the sidewalk, wandering toward Central Square. Just as they composed themselves, a siren pierced the air, the fire station across the street opening up and a big fire

83

truck making its way down Mass Ave. A police cruiser turned on its blue lights and left them flashing.

Sudden sirens no longer triggered Suzanne, but the damn flashing lights drove her eyes crazy. Cutting down a side street, she hurried to get away from the flashes. Kari followed quietly, knowing exactly why Suzanne made the route change, not saying a word. They'd been through this before.

"I," Kari declared in an arch tone, "am totally calling that guy."

"The butt guy or Snake Head?"

"What?"

Suzanne laughed through a mouthful of ice cream. "Sorry," she mumbled.

"You invented nicknames for men I haven't even dated yet?"

"You don't want to date them. You want to sleep with them."

"Same difference."

Suzanne shuddered. "I didn't sleep with my date tonight. Can you believe I ended up on a date with Steve Raleigh?"

Kari frowned. "That name sounds famil—wait! Oh, my God! He's that super pompous guy who was all over Jessica Coffin's Twitter stream when he was dating her, right? Couple years ago? This is all ringing a bell. *He* was your date? I didn't put it together when you called."

Suzanne shrugged. "I didn't research him. Just knew his name was Steve and he worked in the financial sector. Met him in public, so...."

"That's bad?"

"I need to bathe in plane wing degreaser after spending an hour with him."

"Sounds like a rough night."

"You got the phone numbers for two different guys tonight."

"You got kissed."

"Yeah," Suzanne said through a sigh, restraining herself from touching her lips. Gerald. "What am I going to do?"

"Let him make the next move. He certainly owes that to you. All these years, and not a word. He just dumped you?"

Suzanne nodded, eating her sundae. Memory has a funny way of protecting the psyche at all costs. It pulls out every stop, like a mother sensing danger near her child. The will to survive trumps all, and in Suzanne's case, memory protected her heart.

But it wasn't infallible.

"He did. He got his discharge before I did. Sent me an email."

"I know. You told me. A single fucking email, and then he disappeared." Hearing it from Kari's mouth always made it seem as stark as it felt. Confirmation from another person that pain was real made bearing it slightly easier.

"Not his style at all," Suzanne mused. "Never was. Gerald was direct and forthright, completely blunt." She smiled, her mouth twisting with bitter reverie. "It made him perfect for me."

"Because you're the epitome of passive-aggressive," Kari joked.

"We were a pair."

"A powerful pair, I'll bet," Kari said, smiling, giving Suzanne a look only a good friend could give. "You must be reeling."

Suzanne held a full spoon of carbs aloft. "Exhibit #1, your honor."

"And he's a client."

"Not quite." Suzanne paused. "Okay, he is. Sort of. The billionaire's estate handed this portion of his will to our firm. I'm just passing on the information to Gerald."

"He's a client, Suzanne. Don't mince words."

"I'm asking to be reassigned tomorrow. I can't take this."

"And you generally can take a lot."

"I can. But not this. Especially if it drags out. There is no way I can let Gerald Wright back into my life."

"He already is," Kari pointed out, gently.

He already is.

CHAPTER SEVEN

It was hot, the kind of heat that permeates every cell, flowing through you like your bones conduct it. He was a conduit and she was a live wire, the rough press of skin against lips a ritual they'd performed so many times before, a ceremony that should have been routine but that inspired new revelations. Her breast was heavy in his hand, ripe and full, the perfect size for his mouth. Her gasp made him smile against the hollow of her throat as he kissed her, inhaling deeply.

Days.

It had been days since they'd been together, and the desperation clung to their skin like a unique scent. He smelled her need. She tasted him, licking the fine groove between his ribs, her mouth making his abs quiver, his sharp intake of air curling his belly inward. Away.

Sweat rolled off them like water, pure and evoked by the desert heat but vanquished by their mutual need. Her face was flushed by this connection, the way his hand found her between her legs, how his tongue played with her nipple, how she moved to wrap her palm around his shaft and stroked once, twice—just enough before he stopped her, needing more heat.

Wet, wild heat.

Her breath on his hip chilled him, cooler than the ambient temperature, the rise and fall of her chest as the air tickled his slick skin making his body tingle.

As she sank lower, her mouth a fortress, a temple, an asylum, he groaned and pulled her up. Straddling him, *she sank home, her hands sliding up from his navel to his shoulders, her long, blonde hair free and spilling behind her back as she arched.*

The tent felt like nirvana, her body heaven, their union complete as they both—

Gerald awoke with a start, gasping into the strange box of reality, the room dark with shadows and filled with the scent of deeply anticipated horror.

"Oh, God," he grunted, breathing erratic, heart in flames in the center of his chest.

That dream.

That fucking dream.

He hadn't had that dream about Suzanne in eight years.

Drawing on every tool in his psychological coping toolbox, Gerald started with deep breaths. Inhale for eight, exhale for four. Something like that. His hands fisted the sheets, which were damp in sections. Sweating profusely, Gerald stood, throwing the sheet off him, stomping through his bedroom naked, headed to the kitchen for a glass of water.

Instead, he found himself five minutes later, standing in front of the open freezer door.

Just...standing there.

A glance at the stovetop clock told him it was 4:56 a.m. Sunrise soon. The day would begin.

Hell, the day had clearly begun *already*. No way was he going back to bed.

His nose was cold. His back was covered with sweat. One drop trickled down his spine and into his ass crack. And yet, still he stood there, stupidly staring at a half-empty freezer.

Enlightenment would not come from a frozen pad Thai dinner.

Today was his day off. He had a wide-open schedule. Nothing planned.

Which made today dangerous.

Think, man. Think, he urged himself, recalling what his psychologist at the Veterans Affairs center had told him, all those years ago. Use the tools. Don't define yourself by the intrusive thoughts.

He froze.

And realized that the dream had been different this time.

Blinking, he felt his corneas stick against the backs of his eyelids, the rapid eye movement necessary to return his body to the well-oiled machine it needed to be.

The dream was *different*.

Ten years ago, when the invasive dreams had started, they'd ended with him reaching up to her beautiful neck, trying to choke Suzanne. Trying to hurt her. He'd always woken up in the middle of the violence. He'd never actually killed her in the dream.

He'd also never told her about the dreams.

Not a single damn one.

And that's why he broke it off.

Because he never, ever wanted to take the chance that the violence might move from his subconscious to reality.

Four psychologists and two psychiatrists had tried to convince him he never would—in real life—but he knew PTSD could play tricks with your mind. It was a nasty bugger, a second self that took up real estate in the body, a lurker in the shadows that waited to torment you when least expected.

No, he didn't think he'd ever actually hurt Suzanne.

Leaving her made it ironclad. A guarantee.

Until last night, he'd been certain that his decision was the only choice.

Until last night, he hadn't allowed himself to play the regret game.

Until last night, he hadn't let himself hope.

And until last night, he hadn't had that damn dream for eight years.

Bzzz.

He checked his phone. A text from his friend, Vince.

Hey, sleepyhead. Slacker. Get up and come lift with me. I could use a wimp to wipe my brow and fetch towels.

Gerald snorted, running a hand over his shaved head. He'd met Vince years ago. Helped him get an in at Anterdec, where Gerald worked. The guy was hard core.

And a bit of a jerk.

I'm up, asshole. You need a real man to show you how it's done? he typed back. Something in his chest loosened. His shoulders dropped. His stomach growled. The parasympathetic nervous system slowly resumed functioning.

He would be okay today.

He had to be.

If you're the real man, then I fear for humanity's future, Vince typed back. *Bring coconut oil. I ran out.*

What's the coconut oil for? Your blow-up doll? Gerald replied.

Your sister, was Vince's reply.

Gerald barked out an outraged guffaw.

My sister would kick your ass if she read that, Gerald tapped out.

She single? Got pics?

Give me twenty minutes, and don't you ever touch my sister.

But your mother's fair game, Vince typed back.

If you're into necrophilia, pervert. My mom's been dead for five years, Gerald answered.

She single? Got pics?

You're a sick motherfucker, Vince.

Not yet...get your ass here. We got a preener. Need to put him in his place.

Twenty, Gerald typed one-handed as he walked into the bedroom, fishing around in a laundry basket of clean clothes he hadn't put away, finding workout clothes.

Five minutes later, he was on his motorcycle, zooming toward the gym, relieved to have something to do.

Even if it meant hearing Vince talk about dating his lesbian sister.

Especially if it meant hearing Vince talk about dating his sister, not knowing she was gay.

Early morning in Watertown meant uncrowded streets and the near-daylight glow of bluish skies that gave the town the feel of a straight-to-video movie set. He lived three blocks down from where the Boston Marathon bomber had been caught in a boat, bleeding under the cover, ensconced during a fugitive search that Gerald had spent in Boston, shuttling James McCormick everywhere that day.

Like everyone else in the neighborhood, he simultaneously felt deep reverence for the event and an underlying horror at how it had touched his life so closely.

The gym where he and Vince worked out didn't even have a sign. It barely had a ceiling, but the brick warehouse had space. Lots of space, two bathrooms, two locker rooms, and plenty of muscle.

Who needed more than that?

Vince was already in the open gym area, lifting two-hundred-pound sandbags. Three old semi truck tires littered the ground around him. Add in two long, thick ropes and a few kettlebells, and the guy was in his element.

Give him a twelve-foot wall to scale and he would have been giddy.

If Vince did giddy.

"Wimp!" he shouted, drawing a few curious sets of eyes. Vince stood at about six foot four and weighed three hundred pounds, all muscle, bone and sinew. His body was an inverted triangle on top of two thick tree-trunk legs. Covered in tattoos with a long, thick, black braid that hung down the middle of his back like a rope you climbed to get to him, Vince was a mountain.

"Wuss!" Vince called back, working on finding a way to shoulder a sandbag on each shoulder. He hadn't broken a sweat.

Gerald felt the love.

"Get your ass on the rowing machine and warm up. Then get in here and push shit around from one spot to the other." Vince paused and glared. "Bring my coconut oil?"

"I brought you KY jelly. Tastes better."

"Quit talking about sex. That's like dangling a piece of yarn in front of a kitten and never letting them play with it."

"Since when did you start comparing yourself to a kitten, Vince?"

"Since I started dreaming about pussy nonstop."

The comment caught Gerald off guard, his stone face rippling briefly as his heart sped up with the misplaced notion that Vince somehow knew why he was already awake when the text had come in.

"You, too? Man, we're fucking monks, aren't we?"

"You may be fucking monks, Vince, but I don't swing that way."

The guy grunted. "Warm up. Quit talking about your pecker." He frowned. "You got a new woman?"

"An old one." He regretted the words instantly.

"You're sleeping with elderly women now?"

"Ha ha."

"What do you mean, 'an old one'?"

"Nothing."

Vince had a way of stopping and staring at you until it wasn't so much that he pried the truth out of you. Those eyes made the truth cry Uncle and flee.

"I saw an ex of mine."

"When?"

"Yesterday."

"Not Suzanne?" He'd mentioned her over the years.

"Yep."

"How in the hell did that happen?"

"She lives here. In Boston."

"And you just happened to run into her in a city full of hundreds of thousands of people? You're a walking coincidence. Buy a lottery ticket today, man."

"She delivered inheritance papers to me."

Shocking Vince wasn't easy. His face was damn near comical with surprise. "You? Inherit what?"

"Long story."

"I got all day, man."

"Don't want to talk about what I'm inheriting."

"You about to be rich?"

He snorted.

"Then let's talk about Suzanne," Vince continued. "You back together?"

"No."

"You want to be?"

The short inhale, then hitched breath, that took over his body was unscripted.

"I'll take that as a yes," Vince said dryly. "You gonna tell her the truth this time?"

"Fuck off."

"Gerald, man, you gotta tell her."

93

"We're done." Before Vince could respond, Gerald shoved earbuds in and jumped on the old rowing machine. Within two minutes, he was in the zone.

The zone where he couldn't hear Vince.

Old Jorgen, the guy who owned the place, limped between two truck tires and said something to Vince, who paused and turned to give Jorgen his complete attention. Vince would eat a mountain for the guy. Old Jorg was about ninety, with the kind of near-perfect posture in old men that made them pigeon-chested. His hips couldn't hide his age, and he walked a little bowlegged, but otherwise had the stature of a twenty year old.

Jorg had let Vince live in the office when his step-dad kicked him out at fifteen. Gerald hadn't known Vince then. Just knew the tale. Vince had become a personal trainer the old-fashioned way: by being a towel boy for the crazy boxers who came in here. Step by step, he'd fought his way up.

That was literally all Gerald knew about Vince's past.

And Vince seemed to like it that way.

Fine. Gerald wasn't exactly the spill-your-guts type, either. They bonded over torn muscle fibers.

The more, the better.

As Gerald raced through his warm-up, he tore his eyes away from the old man and the beast, listening to the heavy metal pounding through his earbuds. If he closed his eyes, he could recall the image of Suzanne's gloriously nude body.

Hey, there.

Bad idea. The rowing machine suddenly became unbearably uncomfortable.

He looked at Old Jorg and imagined the locker room toilet.

Better.

Understanding why he'd had that dream wasn't exactly rocket science. Stimulus, response.

See Suzanne, dream about her.

But truly grasping why he kissed her—and why she let him—was a puzzle.

He hadn't even opened those damn inheritance papers. Tucked away in his gym bag, he'd thrown them in on a lark. Vince had a keen way of cutting through bullshit to get to the down-and-dirty heart of an issue.

He'd ask him after they moved the equivalent of a skyscraper in weight.

A pinch at his ear and the muted bliss of death metal was interrupted by Vince's hot breath.

"Gotta go. Emergency."

"What's wrong?"

But Vince was gone, the front door swinging, Old Jorg watching with blinking eyes, like an old wrinkled owl.

Shit.

Gerald tucked his worry away, knowing Vince would have told him if he'd wanted to. Instead, he jumped off the rowing machine and made a beeline for Vince's tires.

Might as well flip rubber if he wasn't going to wear any.

Bracing his legs as he lunged down, he lifted the huge, stinking black mass of petroleum, end over end, three times. Glutes screaming, he ignored them. Bodies in motion don't sound like people screaming, thank God.

Self-torture he could handle.

By the time every muscle in his body shook, he was dripping with sweat and no more enlightened, but at least he wasn't plagued by a racing mind with nothing better to do.

Vince came jogging back in just as Gerald sat on a boxer's chair, drinking water.

"Wimped out already?"

"Where'd you go? Tea party?"

"Emergency," Vince said tersely.

"Sorry. Everything okay?"

"Don't wanna talk about it."

"Fine. Don't talk. Lift."

"Too edgy. Spar with me."

Gerald snorted. "I might be a masochist, but I'm not suicidal. I can tell you're stoked. Too much anger. Too much energy. Pick some naive kid in here and beat him. I'm not going in the ring with you."

Vince cursed.

"Run with me, then."

"I'm wiped, man." Plus, whatever had made Vince leave like that loomed over them like a bad spirit, not quite ready to move on.

"Too wiped to run?" Vince walked over to the weight racks and grabbed a vest. He began tucking little weight pouches into the pockets. By Gerald's count, he loaded up eighty pounds.

"Three miles," Gerald said grudgingly.

"That's like getting your dick stroked over the pants, man."

"Excuse me?"

"You're a tease."

"You're comparing being your running partner with *that*?"

"Sex brain, man. I've got it bad."

Bzzz.

Gerald's phone buzzed in his bag, which was on a long bench next to him. He grabbed the phone.

James McCormick.

"My boss? What's one of my bosses doing texting me at six a.m. on my day off?"

"They own your ass, G." Vince began running in place, wearing a hundred-pound vest. "C'mon. Get it done."

Gerald read the text:

I have a medical appointment that has been moved to eight a.m. Pick me up at my residence.

The guy got to the point.

Yes, sir, he typed back. *Received.*

"I gotta work early," Gerald said with a sigh, half relieved not to need to run, half sad to have to drive James McCormick to the cancer center. For the past half a year, Gerald had managed his boss's appointments, which the elder McCormick hid from his sons. The old man asked him to keep it quiet, and Gerald was the only one he trusted to see him in a weakened state.

"G, it's your day off."

"Not anymore."

"Fishing for a reason to leave?"

"No. James McCormick needs me for an eight o'clock medical appointment." He knew he could take a different day off this week. The old man would never say it, but he needed Gerald—and only Gerald—for this errand.

"Haven't met him yet." Vince grunted. "Andrew's decent." He frowned. "Medical, huh? Is it serious?"

Vince's casual tone, calling Andrew McCormick, CEO of Anterdec, Inc., by his first name, made Gerald shake his head.

"How do you get away with that? Andrew McCormick insists I call him sir." Changing the subject meant preserving confidentiality.

"Charisma. Either you've got it, or you're a loser."

"You misspoke, Vince. You meant to say *bullshit*."

Vince grabbed a medicine ball and pitched it at Gerald's head. Gerald ducked. The thwock of the weight against the padded wall sounded like a gut punch.

"What was your emergency, Vince?"

"My dad."

Gerald sucked in air sharply. "He's bugging you again?" Once Vince began making steady money as a trainer, his deadbeat dad came back into the picture. Junkies love success.

"Yeah. This time, he OD'd."

"He in the hospital?"

Vince's braid swung across his back as he shook his head. "Nah. Refused transport. One of his junkie buddies knows I work out here, so..."

"I'm sorry."

Vince gave him the hairy eyeball. "Go to work for the billionaires, Mr. Heir. Just remember we peons when you're rolling in it."

Ducking just in time, he laughed and shot through the front doors, wondering if he could beat rush hour traffic to get to Anterdec in time for a shower before his shift began.

As he left, he caught Vince's eye, the look serious.

And then he remembered the inheritance papers in his bag.

It was going to be a long day.

A very, very long day.

CHAPTER EIGHT

"I've never seen you behave so unprofessionally, Suzanne. What happened to the iron maiden? You've been rock solid for seven years. Hell, half the junior associates are convinced you're part robot." Norman Phelps, one of the law firm's founders, glared at her from his desk. Remaining seated, wearing half-glasses, he looked up over the edge of both lenses with the air of a well-fed old man who doesn't have time for anything but his own agenda.

Eight a.m. was too early for this. Suzanne took a long, hot sip from her black coffee and watched him over the rim of her cup, trying to decide how to respond.

With aggression, or *more* aggression?

"The fact that I've worked here for seven years without a single personal request like this should be a testament to my robotic nature, Norm." She glared back. Suzanne wasn't taking crap from anyone. This was anemic compared to the face-offs she'd had over the years from opposing counsel, various judges, and at times, her own firm colleagues.

Norm needed to try harder.

Suzanne wanted someone other than Gerald and herself to be pissed off at.

"I can't take you off the Hopewell-Wright case, Suzanne."

"Can't or won't?"

"Doesn't matter."

"The difference matters to me."

"I said it doesn't matter."

"Then how about I take my client base and find a firm where it does matter?"

Never before had she made the threat. She'd thought it, sure, plenty of times over the past year, since making partner. Not quite a year—eleven months.

"I literally cannot take you off the case." Phelps looked at the open door, and to Suzanne's amazement (which she hid carefully), he stood, crossed the room, and shut the door with a barely audible click that felt like a signature in blood on a contract from hell.

When he turned to face her, his eyes were tired. Norm Phelps wasn't the most attractive of men (at least, to Suzanne), with hair the color of a young lion, artfully colored on a regular basis, and overly-white teeth that glowed as a result of his burnt-orange tan.

But he wasn't an asshole, either.

She had to remind herself of that fact daily. Take nothing personally, his executive legal secretary, Inez, had told Suzanne on her first day. Not one single word.

"Look. The Hopewell case is sensitive. We're in a nasty grey area with this one."

"Grey area?" Phelps, Miller and Lin didn't do grey areas. Nothing but black and white. She stiffened. "Are you asking me to act in ways that could compromise my license?"

"God, no, Suzanne." He sighed, pinching the bridge of his nose, lifting his reading glasses up over his eyebrows. "You know I would never do that."

"That's not quite true. Remember the Kikendaal case?"

His sigh deepened.

"And the Brownlea, and the—"

"Fine. Fine. Let's just say that your friend—"

"Ex-fiancé."

"Your ex is inheriting one hell of a mess."

Protectiveness for Gerald kicked in. "What?"

"It's an artifact."

"I know that."

"A very rare artifact. A pre-Buddhist item that was supposed to have been destroyed by the Taliban."

She frowned. "What?"

"And allegedly carries a curse." He rolled his tongue in his cheek, jaw tightening.

"Phelps, now I know you're pulling my leg. This isn't a joke." She let out a derisive snort.

He paled.

"I know. I'm not the type to get caught up in stupid New-Agey crap like this. But Harold Hopewell was clear: Phelps, Miller handles the case, and Suzanne Dayton is the point person. Period. The archaeologist from the MFA will be here at two p.m. for the meeting."

"Meeting?" She gave him a blank look.

He waved a dismissive hand. "Letitia must have put it in your calendar."

"Letitia is my paralegal. Not my assistant."

"Oh. Right. That's Margaret." He shook his head quickly, as if re-centering.

Norm wasn't usually this off. "What's wrong?" she asked, as neutrally as possible.

"Nothing."

"Margaret has been my admin for three years, Norm. You don't magically forget someone like that."

He swallowed, hard, the shell rolling off him, revealing the deeper man. The nervous glance at the door made her internal danger radar go off.

"This conversation didn't happen."

How bad was this?

"Of course not."

"Look, the Hopewell case is a hot potato. The fact that your ex is an heir is a sick bit of bad luck."

101

"We're making decent billable hours off it," Suzanne reminded him.

"And the terms of the will state that you, and you alone, must handle the case."

She laughed. "Good one. That won't hold up in court."

Alarm filled his face. "We can't take this anywhere near a court!"

She narrowed her eyes. "I think we'd better stop right here, Norm, and you'd damn well better explain what this is all about."

Curses? Pre-Buddhist artifacts? The Taliban?

And what the hell did Gerald have to do with any of it?

"If you don't, I resign. I know how many billable hours I bring into the firm. You guys need me. So spill."

"The artifact is a rare religious item. Dates back centuries, likely millennia. Between age, historical value, political value, actual precious metal and gemstone content, and the competition to own it, that damn item may be worth a cool hundred million on the black market, Suzanne."

Well.

She'd demanded the truth.

And now she had it.

Plunking her stunned ass into a chair, Suzanne's coffee dripped out of the small opening on the top as the cup slammed into the tabletop. "Gerald's inheriting a hundred million dollar artifact? *Gerald*?" She bit back the phrase *my Gerald* just in time.

He wasn't hers.

Even if she could still conjure the taste of that kiss last night.

"He's inheriting a legal and political nightmare. But the guy has no choice. It's his fault."

"What?"

"Have you read the file? The full file?"

"Yes."

Phelps pulled a fat envelope out of his jacket pocket. "Good. Then you're ready for this."

She took the envelope and began to open it. "What's in here?"

"The rest of the story." He tossed the envelope on the thick mahogany-topped desk. "Read it."

She picked it up and took a step toward the door.

"No. In here."

Suzanne looked at him in disbelief. "I can only read the documents in here? In your office?"

"Those papers do not leave the room. They're not part of the official record. None of this is. Hell, the actual artifact doesn't officially *exist*."

Alarm buzzed through her bones. "I'm definitely removing myself from this case."

"Suzanne," he said softly. Norm Phelps was anything but soft. "Read. Then decide."

Against her better nature, she pulled the thick batch of papers from the envelope and unfolded them.

And then she read.

And read.

And gaped.

Her coffee was cold when she reached for it, drinking anyhow. After she chugged the entire enormous cup, she looked at Norm. "These papers say that eleven years ago, Gerald Wright stole a very rare religious and cultural artifact from Afghanistan, smuggled it into the U.S., and somehow it landed in the hands of Harold Hopewell."

"'Stole' isn't the right word."

"What is?"

"'Rescued.' Keep reading."

She flipped through the papers, speed reading.

Her eyes halted abruptly on a name she hadn't read or heard in ten years.

"'Harrison Kulli!'" Her voice cracked. "Jesus, Norm. What the hell does he have to do with any of this?"

Norm shook his head, the skin around his eyes sagging like a depressed bloodhound. "You knew him, right? In the Navy?"

She looked up sharply. "How did you know?"

"Research. Investigations. Background checks." He gave her a one-shoulder shrug.

"You mean corporate spying."

"Details."

"Gerald smuggled this artifact to the U.S.? When?"

"On some sort of trip to D.C. It gets murky from there. Somehow it ended up in a private collection owned by Harold Hopewell."

"And now Hopewell left it to Gerald as an inheritance?"

Norm nodded, sighing deeply.

"Where is it?"

"The artifact?"

"No. The Hope Diamond. Yes, the artifact."

"It is in an undisclosed location."

"You're acting like this is some kind of summer action thriller, Norm. Why all the cloak-and-dagger crap?"

"Because it's a cursed religious artifact made of gold, encrusted with rare jewels, and it has a black market value of a hundred million or so, give or take eight figures."

Suzanne just blinked.

"Gerald inherited this."

"Yes. And part of our job is to convince him to sell it."

"Sell it? He can't! It has to be given back to the rightful government. International law dictates exactly what he needs to do."

Norm's discomfort level shot through the roof. She could feel it radiating off him like toxic paint fumes. "Technically, no. This artifact was never recorded by a cultural institution or government body. It doesn't exist. But even more important: handing it back to the government would lead to its destruction."

"Under the Taliban, sure, but not under the elected government of Afghanistan."

He gave her a gimlet eye. "You're not that naive, Suzanne. You know damn well that a pre-Buddhist religious artifact like this, with so much significance, would be destroyed. Or melted down and sold. It wouldn't even reach the government, no matter how hard we might try. The channel to get from A to B would be rife with interlopers."

Suzanne studied a picture of the item. It was solid gold, a statue of a small woman with large breasts and a protruding belly, a tiny version of a human coming out of her as she gave birth.

"Inside the statue there's an enormous emerald and a ruby, and legend says that if the gold is melted down with great care, on one of the layers there is a map, etched into the gold, leading to unlocking Indus script."

She snorted. "C'mon. Now I know you're messing with me. Who am I supposed to meet with today? Nicolas Cage and Harrison Ford?"

"No. Gerald Wright and the archaeologist we're trying to sniff out to examine the artifact in question."

"If what you're saying is true, this relic could be something like a Rosetta Stone?"

He nodded.

Dumbfounded. She was dumbfounded.

"Wait. Where is it? An item like this should be under lock and key, with armored guards! This is ridiculous."

"But it's true. And the item is at Hopewell's Boston home, protected by a security team."

The weight of the paperwork fooled her into thinking this wasn't as great a burden as it truly was. Norm's explanation, this cloak-and-dagger behavior, left her suspicious and reeling.

"Then you should understand how serious this is. Our position, by the way, is to encourage Gerald Wright to sell."

"Sell?"

"Sell the artifact. Quickly. Get out from under the item. He's a chauffeur and an art teacher. Impress on him that the money is life-altering, We already have someone who represents a client. They have an open offer on the table of fifty million."

"A buyer?" she repeated dumbly.

"Yes. Represented by Harrison Kulli. I believe it's in the paperwork."

"Harrison Kulli wants to *buy* the artifact from Gerald?" This was getting crazier and crazier by the minute.

"On the behalf of a client of his, yes."

"Harrison Kulli has a client? A client for what?"

"Kulli represents an anonymous buyer."

"I'll bet he does. Bad pennies always turn up."

Norm frowned. "What's the deal with him, Suz? Why's he bother you so much?"

"He was my commanding officer in Afghanistan."

Norm was in the middle of eating a donut and froze. "And?"

"Do you not understand why this is setting off my hinky meter?"

He made a small huffing sound, then resumed stuffing his face. "Your ex-fiancé has just inherited an artifact that your former commanding officer is trying to buy for a client. For fifty million dollars."

"Just another day at the office."

He frowned, giving her an evaluative look. "It wasn't a coincidence that Phelps, Miller was chosen to handle this particular bequest, was it?"

Suzanne broke eye contact, the paper resting in her hand like a weapon.

"I don't think so. But what does it mean?"

"It means I need to chase down Miller and have a talk. But it also means you're still on the case."

"For now."

He gave her a small, concessionary head nod. "For now."

The air between them changed. She couldn't give it a name, but the essence of this case—what was supposed to be a simple bequest, handled like any other—had shifted.

So had the balance of power.

* * *

"Want to grab some Thai for lunch, Suz?" Letitia asked, looking up from her bar exam study guide. Four long years at Suffolk University night school and Letitia had just finished law school. Suzanne had warned her that was the easy part.

Letitia had just laughed. Now, three months into studying for the bar, she wasn't laughing so much. Most lunches were about studying, so Suzanne had already made plans.

"I have a date, actually," Suzanne answered, quickly skimming her email, organizing by label. Zero inbox was her goal, and so far, she was holding steady.

"A date? With who? Not Steve whats-his-face again?" Letitia let out a whoop of amusement.

"No. This time, it's with a fellow dog owner."

"You're choosing guys by whether they own a dog or not?"

"It's this new dating service. Ever heard of DoggieDate?"

"No."

Suzanne shrugged and kept her eyes on the screen. "It's for people with dogs. You find fellow dog lovers and see if you're compatible."

"The humans, or the dogs?"

"Both."

"Whatever happened to just meeting a hot guy in a bar, sleeping with him, and slowly falling in love?"

Suzanne looked up. "I'm all for that. Where do I sign up?"

"Not at some crazy dating company that matches you by dog. What kind of dog does this guy have? And since when did Smoochy become your wingman?"

"Smoochy is not my—oh, damn. You're right."

"You're using a dog to score dates."

"I'm using my dog to help me *find* the right date."

"No difference."

"Huge difference."

They laughed. Both were single, and both shared the pain of finding someone in Boston.

"Hey, I don't judge," Letitia said in a voice that made it clear she most certainly did.

"You're the one who found a long-term boyfriend on craigslist," Suzanne said drolly.

"Until I learned he wanted me to have six sister wives back in Montana. And that I'd have to change my name to Tuesday."

Some days that didn't sound so bad.

"Well, hopefully this guy isn't a pervert. He owns a beagle named Joe."

"What is it with people who name their dogs real names? You got it right," Letitia said, shaking her head. "I can't imagine having a cat named Fred or a dog named James."

"Smoochy wasn't my choice. That's what Elizabeth named her."

"Then Elizabeth has common sense."

Suzanne gave her a half-wave and escaped. When Letitia got going and was eyeballs-deep in bar exam prep, she could work herself into a rant.

The fast walk two blocks from her office to the food court where she was meeting a Chandler Hopkins, 34, software developer for a multi-national nutrition company website who loved dogs, wasn't enough time to process her meeting with Norm.

And the name Harrison Kulli had been like chewing aluminum foil with a mouthful of fillings.

That rat bastard.

The guy had weaseled his way into every mess possible in Afghanistan, including inappropriate sexual behavior with local Afghan women. Rumor had it he'd stolen local relics and sold them on the black market. The guy had been a DJ before the war.

And now he worked for wealthy clients who wanted to buy rare artifacts?

The language in the paperwork confused her. Gerald had somehow rescued a rare pre-Buddhist sculpture made from gold and jewels, one with a history predating known records? He'd never said a word to her. They'd been together then, too, during the dates noted in Hopewell's letters. Gerald had smuggled the item into the U.S. and somehow helped get it in the hands of people who would respect it, and not strip it of its cultural value by melting it down and selling it off.

Which was exactly what Kulli would do.

So many questions. How had Gerald gotten his hands on it? How had he hidden it? What kind of defensive maneuvers had he engaged in to get it out of Kulli's hands? A rule-follower by nature, Gerald wasn't the type to commit federal felonies willy-nilly, and yet as Suzanne thought it through, they were racking up in her mind.

Motivation was a powerful force.

Almost as strong as love.

The question of the relic itself was intriguing, too. While Afghanistan was Islamic now, it had been predominantly Buddhist before that, and before Buddhism the area had been filled with a mixture of ancient religions. Rich with possibilities—and not just financial—the relic could hold the key to unlocking so much about mankind's past.

The Indus river valley civilization was one of the first civilizations of mankind. Modern-day Afghanistan was at the far reaches of the ancient society. For Gerald to have found such an item, smuggled it to the U.S. without her knowing, and now to be her client, an heir to the very item, made her mind boggle.

The entire case felt too big. Too bizarre. Too unreal.

Yet it was all *too* real.

She hadn't been looking forward to the two p.m. meeting with Gerald. Quite the opposite. But now that she knew more about the case, a thrill shot through her. While the romantic aspect of her relationship with Gerald was an emotional land mine, the details of this inheritance were her job. Asking—and getting answers—would give her insight into life ten years ago.

Phelps mentioned the belief that the item was cursed. She'd snorted, but now she wondered. What did that mean?

She entered the cool, bracing air of the indoor air filtration system and a bank of escalators greeted her. As she rode up, she cleared her head, hitting reboot on her emotions.

Chandler. She was about to meet Chandler.

Every first date she forced herself to go on felt like a micro-aggression against herself. Finding love the old-fashioned way, through coincidence and circumstance, was so much more preferable. That's how she'd met Gerald—by sheer accident.

Then again, look how that had turned out.

"Suzanne?"

Caught up in her own thoughts, she realized she'd walked right past a man in a business suit, sitting at a small metal table, looking right at her with a steely attention that put her on guard. Closely cropped brown hair, a little lighter at the temples, with honey-brown eyes that impossibly matched his hair color. He was freshly shaven and smelled like wet soap when she shook his hand, his eyes remaining on hers though she had the clear sense that he would have preferred to catalog her body.

She would not have minded.

He was tall. At least six foot six, and even in her high heels he towered over her. Broad-shouldered with a big body made for double-breasted suits, he was a force, radiating power.

"Chandler?"

His face cracked with a smile that met his eyes.

"Got it in one go."

"Excuse me?"

"I guessed right on the first shot. I'll take that as a good omen."

She smiled.

He gestured toward a small bistro, tucked away in a side hallway, away from the other restaurant counters. She'd never noticed it before.

"I apologize for not asking you somewhere more intimate, but time is of the essence," he explained, body language loosening as his gaze tightened. His fingertips brushed the small of her back and she used every internal resource at her disposal not to shiver with delight.

When was the last time a man triggered this kind of response from her body?

Oh.

Right.

Gerald. Last night.

Once they were seated at a white-clothed table, surrounded by stemware and dark polished wood, Suzanne found herself gazing into the eyes of one of the most attractive men she had ever seen. Chandler Hopkins could have been a model. He came out of a black-and-white, nuanced Ralph Lauren ad. She could imagine him seven stories tall on a blinking screen in Times Square.

And he was *cataloguing* her.

After he ordered a lovely red wine she enjoyed more than she should, they settled in to salads. Ten minutes into the conversation and she knew he was from Wisconsin, that he had graduated from the University of Chicago with a degree in art history, and that he was obsessed with WikiLeaks and Edward Snowden.

He didn't ask a single question about her.

"What's Joe like?" she asked politely, trying not to stare at his hands, which were manicured and better looking than hers. She wasn't the nail polish type for herself, but she suddenly wanted a manicure. His hands were just so pretty.

Talking about dogs seemed like a safe enough conversation topic.

"He's great. Fifth dog in the line in my family. My grandmother had the first Joe. I'm honored to keep the

112

tradition going." His eyes never left her as he spoke. "I read on your profile that you like to use leashes. What about harnesses?" His eyes twinkled with merriment.

"Um, I really don't use harnesses. I think the leash is enough. It gives just enough pressure to make it clear where the boundaries are." She didn't add that Smoochy was so well behaved she rarely needed to even use the leash, but she knew that in the dog world, admitting that was like saying you didn't put your toddler in a car seat.

"And what about discipline?"

As she was about to answer, the server delivered her salmon and his bass. They dug in. Her phone buzzed with a text.

"Pardon me," she said apologetically, reaching into her purse.

"Comes with the territory. I understand. But you'll turn it off when the leash comes out, of course?"

She was immersed in the text from Letitia and wasn't quite sure she'd heard that right. She flashed him a polite smile. "Of course." Maybe he had a strict policy about silencing his phone while walking his dog.

After typing back a quick reply for Letitia to manage a glitch in a probate court issue, Suzanne took a bite of her salmon. Perfect.

The next few minutes were all about eating, sipping wine, and getting used to being silent in snippets around a new guy.

Promising. This was looking promising, though the lack of reciprocal interest had her on edge.

Maybe DoggieDate wasn't such a bad idea after all. Kari had told her about it—the mystery shopping company she worked for had lost the account to a competitor—and Suzanne had made a profile there just last week.

Chandler's quick response and request for a lunch date had been a welcome break from all the dick pics and requests for hookups that came with most sites.

But he was only talking about the dogs now, and that made her wonder.

"How do you handle elimination?" he asked smoothly, as if they were talking about retirement account investment allocations.

"Elimination?"

"Yes. Do you glove up? Bag the waste?" He leaned in, his Patek Philippe watch glittering as a skylight ushered in rays of sunshine after clouds parted. Funny how that status symbol followed quirky guys. "Or do you use dog diapers?" He whispered the last two words with reverence, then licked his lower lip.

She recoiled, the bite of salmon in her mouth suddenly tasting like mulch.

"You—I—well, I use a glove and bags. Always," she added. Was this some kind of purity test to see if she was a responsible dog owner?

"And a muzzle?"

"No. Never! Why would I do that?"

His face fell.

"Sometimes it's necessary, especially when a puppy is being very, very bad." His eyes widened and he took a big swig of his wine.

The way he said *bad* made her spine tingle, and not in an arousing way.

The date just went from *promising* to *rescue text* in three minutes.

A new record.

"Do you have a picture of Joe?" she asked suddenly, eager for any option that took them out of this disturbing discussion.

"No. Why would I carry a picture of my dog in my wallet?" The look he gave her said she was the crazy one. Disarmingly charming and decidedly manipulative, Chandler's ability to make her feel an array of emotions set off alarms.

It was one thing to be attracted to a guy and lose internal control.

It was another to have him keep the ground beneath her emotional feet shifting constantly.

"Let's get down to business," he said, as Suzanne put her knife and fork down, stomach in rebellion, all hope of salvaging the date long gone. She couldn't put her finger on it, but the conversation had turned in such a way that she was done.

"Yes?"

Business? Was he another networker like Steve? Regrouping, she put on her badass hat and made a mental note to reach out to Kari for another ice cream run tonight. Sheesh.

"You have something I want. I have something you want. We could have a fine relationship meeting each other's needs."

Blunt. She had to give him credit for being blunt.

"Other than the muzzle issue, I like your style, Suzanne." He reached for her hand, his thumb caressing the broad line into the wrist. "I like a woman who knows how to control her puppy."

He kept calling Smoochy a puppy. Strange.

"I don't really need to control dogs. As long as they behave, it's easy," she said, using a casual tone but measuring her words carefully.

"And if they don't behave?" The stroking turned warm, his hand heating up. The pulse at the base of his throat started throbbing so hard she could see a blue bulge of vein. He swallowed. Was he starting to sweat?

"I don't know. I'd put them in their crate."

"Yes," he answered, the word like a hiss. Chandler shifted in his seat, pupils dilating.

115

The guy was getting aroused talking about dogs?

"And then what, Suzanne? What if you had a puppy who wouldn't stop sniffing your crotch?"

She stood so fast her napkin went flying up and knocked over her partially-full glass of wine, which tipped toward him. A drop rolled across the table, like a line of blood, soaked into the cloth before it could hit the edge on his side.

"What are you talking about?" she snapped. People turned to stare at the commotion. Chandler's eyes went flinty cold, his nostrils flaring.

He did not stand.

"Sit. Now."

"I'm not a dog you can order around!" she protested, reaching down for her purse and resuming eye contact. Instinct kicked in. Not flight, though she was about to leave.

Fight.

Don't back down. Call him out. Override the fear.

He flushed. Not from embarrassment, but damn—he was *turned on.*

"Please sit down."

"No. I'm done." She turned on her heel, not even certain why this was over, but absolutely convinced that leaving was the right choice.

He followed. She no longer cared about the bill, or the scene they were making, or anything else. Escape was paramount. The guy was off.

"Suzanne, I believe there's been a mistake," he said from behind her, and then he made a mistake.

A *big* mistake.

He grabbed her arm.

Her elbow met his solar plexus with the kind of artistic grace and perfect timing that made the split-second connection an object of beauty, its own entity independent of time and space.

116

The sound Chandler made echoed through the bowels of hell.

"Wha?" he gasped as Suzanne unlocked her knees, spinning around, ready to take him down.

Even in heels.

He held his palms toward her in supplication even as he tried to fold at the waist.

"Not hurting you! Not! Not!" he barked.

Literally barked.

Chandler said those words, then *barked*.

"Arf. Woof," he said under his breath, eyes widening as if he were signaling Suzanne.

But it was all just noise.

"You're crazy," she said.

"Why are you acting like you don't understand what I'm saying?"

"Because I don't speak Bark, Chandler."

"You're a puppy trainer."

Suzanne stared at him.

"A what?"

"Your profile. It said you were into puppy dates."

"So?"

He looked at her like she was stupid. "So...that's code."

"Code?"

A ripple of uncertainty filled his eyes. "You know. The code. The code for puppy play."

"Puppy play?"

"You signed on to be a puppy trainer."

"I don't have those skills. I've never worked with dogs before. I'm a trust and estate lawyer, Chandler. Not someone who breeds dogs or runs obedience classes." What a strange mix up. Her profile was clear about being a lawyer.

He shivered, one corner of his mouth going up.

"Wait a minute." She started to put the pieces together. Obedience. Bad dog. The, uh...questions about elimination. "What, exactly, do you mean by the term 'puppy play'?"

That grin.

"Oh, Suzanne. You're quite the commanding woman. I can tell you know how to make a disobedient puppy turn into a good, well-trained dog."

She just blinked.

"And I'll pay handsomely for it."

"You want to pretend you're a dog and that I'm your owner?"

"Trainer, owner..." His voice dropped. "Name your price."

Oh, God.

"I thought we were here on a date because we both love dogs!" she protested.

He gave her a lascivious grin. "We are."

"OUT! I'm out," she shouted, right in the middle of the food court, blindly stumbling toward the brightest bank of windows she could find. Heart racing, brain scrambled, Suzanne walked quickly to the main doors, relieved by the petroleum-filled air that the streets of downtown Boston pumped steadily through the city.

Horns and shouts, people and engines, all the sounds mingled into background noise that was preferable to being asked about—

She shuddered.

DoggieDate, huh?

She was done.

Absolutely *done* with online dating.

Bzzz.

Her cell phone.

Reminder: 1 p.m. meeting with James McCormick.
Reminder: 2 p.m. meeting with Gerald Wright.

The clock read 12:30 p.m. Just enough time to get to McCormick's house for whatever was going on. James McCormick hadn't specified why he wanted to meet with her, but she assumed it had to do with his late wife's family trust.

Then back to the office for this roller coaster of a day.

Somehow, Chandler Hopkins managed to make her date last night with Steve Raleigh look like a damn romancefest.

Kari was going to die laughing over this one. *Die.*

Someday this would be funny.

Right now, though, she just needed a shower, a large coffee, and to delete her DoggieDate profile.

Permanently.

Chapter Nine

"**M**orning, Mr. McCormick," Gerald said, opening the door to the SUV limo.

James glared at the black beast of a car. "Andrew has some of the strangest ideas about luxury," he grumbled as he climbed in, settling in the middle seat, reaching for the coffee Gerald had procured for the old man.

"Sir?"

"Gerald, do you like driving these SUVs?"

Gerald knew James McCormick was not actually soliciting his opinion. Recently, Anterdec's CEO and James McCormick's son, Andrew, had phased out the older limousines and replaced them with SUVs. The elder McCormick hated the change.

Then again, the man hated *any* change, unless it involved an increase in profits.

"I do, sir, but I also enjoy driving anything but a tank, and asphalt is a luxury."

James laughed, the sound genuine.

"I would imagine anyone who served our fine country in a combat zone would feel that way, Gerald."

Gerald liked the old guy, even if he was an arrogant, pompous jerk sometimes. People were complex. No one was perfect. And as a character study, Gerald found him fascinating. Most of the people he saw the elder McCormick interact with either loved him, hated him, or tried to get something from him.

"Yes, sir. You said Dana Farber?" The famous cancer center in Boston was the location for the last two months of appointments.

The brown eyes that met his in the rearview mirror were filled with anger. "Yes," he said, as if the word itself meant admitting defeat.

"Yes, sir." Gerald moved the enormous SUV down the street like it was a sedan, enjoying the power of the V8 engine. Andrew McCormick had swapped out all of Anterdec's traditional limousines just last month, finally getting rid of the handful the company had kept for the elder McCormick. Gerald had shined James McCormick on. He much preferred the SUVs.

The window glass was stronger, the privacy at a higher threshold, and security was easier.

Gerald wasn't just a chauffeur, after all.

He was a bodyguard as well. James McCormick insisted on hiring drivers with special military backgrounds. Lance, one of the other drivers, had worked for a Blackwater-like private security company before joining the Anterdec team. Two other drivers, José and Tim, rounded out the team who drove the three top Anterdec executives.

Make that two top Anterdec execs.

Declan was gone now.

"Becky?" he heard McCormick say into his phone. "Get me the PR department. I need to schedule a meeting with them to think of ways we can exploit my son's pending wedding. No, not that son. He's already married. I'm talking about Andrew. We need a spike like we got from that crazy helicopter escape. Assemble the PR team for a brainstorming session to come up with ideas. What? No! Absolutely not," he barked into the phone. "Andrew is not to be consulted. It will be presented to him as a *fait accompli*."

Click.

McCormick let out a sound of disgust. "Damn kids. They really don't understand how good they have it." Gerald swore he heard a touch of South Boston in those words.

"Sir?"

A deep *harumph* was his only reply.

Gerald smothered a grin. What James McCormick didn't know was that Andrew McCormick was currently busy making plans with his fiancée, Amanda, that subverted his father. The two had zero interest in turning their wedding into a media spectacle.

Take two giant egos like Andrew and James and put them in conflict.

This would be better than watching *Batman vs. Superman*.

And Gerald had a front-seat view.

Literally.

McCormick tapped on his phone and began speaking. "You're lining up all the media coverage, yes? No, the wedding's not planned until 2018. That's right. How the hell is it my concern whether we can schedule that far in advance, Brona? Make it happen. Clear Litraeon so we can have an escape hatch if needed. I'll work on getting Amanda's mother to do something media-worthy."

As James McCormick barked out orders, Gerald smothered yet another smile. Pam Warrick, from what little exposure Gerald had to the woman, was about as likely to create a media drama as Marie Jacoby was to fade quietly into the background.

The rest of the drive involved a series of calls to investment bankers. McCormick used every second in the limo to conduct business. Just like Andrew. When did these guys get downtime?

The trip from James McCormick's Back Bay home to Dana Farber was fairly short, and by the time he pulled the SUV up to the special entrance, it was 8:35 a.m.

"Ten minutes early. Might as well get it over with." As James McCormick exited the SUV, he gave Gerald a grave look. "Three hours or so, like last time. You'll escort me home."

Last time McCormick looked like death warmed over. Gerald had stayed with him until he fell asleep, sworn to secrecy. "Would you like for me to run errands? Do any shopping while I wait?"

"No."

The guy didn't even bother to turn around as the clipped syllable floated back to Gerald.

No big deal.

He was used to it.

As Gerald pulled away from the private entrance, he mentally scanned the SUV. Gas tank half full; fill it. Car hadn't been washed in five days but was clean. He pulled into a commercial car wash where Anterdec had an account, and listened to classic rock for twenty minutes while the car was washed. Interior detailing took place back at the underground garage at headquarters on a rotation schedule, so he didn't need to worry about that.

McCormick would come out of the appointment asking for a ginger beer (non-alcoholic) and in need of lemon tea. Meeting the creature-comfort needs of billionaires wasn't particularly difficult, but you needed to be on top of logistics at all times.

Who better than a former Navy SEAL to manage *that*?

His personal mobile phone buzzed.

Reminder: inheritance meeting 2 p.m.

Right. He hadn't forgotten. But he still hadn't actually read the paperwork in his gym bag. Why would Harold Hopewell leave a damn thing to someone like

Gerald? The only billionaires he knew were the McCormicks, and he collected a paycheck from them.

Not a trust fund check.

Pulling into the Anterdec underground garage, Gerald waved to Miles, the security guard at the private entrance. Miles was a fellow vet, but thirty years older. Vietnam.

As he set the gas pump on automatic, Gerald let the gallons fly and finally opened the letter Suzanne had given him last night.

The words blurred.

Artifact.

Harold Hopewell.

Precious item saved from the black market.

Integrity.

Bequeathed to you for your service and honor.

As an artist, you understand the deeper value...

Gerald reeled. The words blurred because blood rushed to his temples, the streak of shock riding from ass to earlobes, setting him on guard.

This had to be a joke, right?

And then he saw the name. That damn name.

Harrison Kulli.

His eyes narrowed, the words coming into sharp focus.

He read on, the letter becoming less formal, a personal note from Hopewell himself.

"The same man who tried to steal the artifact and sell it on the black market may return, like a bad penny, to disrupt the transfer of ownership from my estate to you, Gerald. Eleven years ago, your stalwart work in preserving this treasure was critical. I am well aware of the measures you took—legal and illegal—to bring this sacred item to a place of safety, from the scheming hands of those who would desecrate it. Do not be surprised by

Harrison Kulli's reappearance at this juncture. As before, I trust you will thwart his efforts."

As his teeth shifted suddenly, Gerald realized he was grinding them, jaw tight as an alligator's with prey in it.

Kulli.

That bastard.

Speed reading through the rest, he heard the click of a gas pump in the distance. Tank full. Real life moved on, second by second, action by action as he took in the future and the past in one single sheaf of pages.

Kulli. Suzanne. The artifact. The mental list of work errands he had to run. All the tiny life issues he juggled in the back of his mind.

And then there was the emotional response of all the carefully glued-together pieces of his soul.

One second at a time, he reminded himself.

You live one second at a time.

Even if it feels like they're all dumped on you at once.

Bzzz.

Work phone.

James McCormick.

Come back now, is all the text said.

Yes, sir, he replied automatically, stuffing the inheritance papers in his front jacket pocket, a cold dread filling him. He'd never been summoned back to the hospital so quickly for the elder McCormick.

This wouldn't be good.

For months, the old man had hidden his true condition from his kids. What little he shared with Gerald made it hard to gauge. The cycle seemed to be treatment, fatigue, recovery.

Gerald never asked. Wasn't in his job description. He took orders, watched for danger, and worked to make the lives of the McCormick men as glitch-free as possible.

126

In return, they didn't ask him questions about his life, either.

A good bargain.

Back at Dana Farber fifteen minutes later, Gerald live-parked and marched straight for the reception desk. Years ago he'd learned that the same skills used in managing recruits—namely, to pretend you had ultimate authority—worked well on people whose job was simply to point the way.

Five minutes later, he was in a private room with James McCormick, who looked like someone had drained all the blood out of him.

"Excuse me," said a small woman with a shock of grey hair amidst thick, dark brown waves. "Are you Mr. McCormick's son?"

Both Gerald and James McCormick looked scandalized at the thought.

"No. I'm his chauffeur." Not quite true, but that was the face they showed to the world.

Her demeanor changed, an injection of sympathy in the look she gave McCormick. "I see. Then patient confidentiality means that I cannot comment on his condition."

"He's fine," McCormick grunted.

She gave Gerald a no-nonsense look. "James had an adverse reaction, so we're halting treatment today." She patted McCormick's hand. "It happens."

"It hasn't happened to me before," McCormick said weakly.

"Self-care for the next week is mandatory." She looked at Gerald. "We gave him some anti-anxiety and anti-nausea medication. He shouldn't be left alone for the next twelve to twenty-four hours."

"Quit talking about me like I'm not in the room. I'm fine," McCormick snapped.

"Your labs say otherwise, Mr. McCormick," the doctor announced. She shrugged and left.

He made a dismissive noise. "Let's go," the old man said, gruff and angry.

"Sir?"

McCormick began to stand, then keeled to the right in an alarming fashion. By his side in seconds, Gerald grabbed him in time, keeping him upright.

"I could use a sit-down," McCormick said, as if he were asking for a martini. With great care, Gerald spent the next ten minutes moving him to the main foyer, then out to the SUV. It was like moving a box you can't lift, one shove at a time, except Gerald had to be gentle.

"I hate these machines," McCormick growled as Gerald worked to find the smoothest way in. He had to give McCormick credit; it was much easier helping a sick person into a traditional limousine vs. an SUV.

"Home." The simple word carried so much.

"Sir, should I call one of your sons to help—"

"No! Absolutely not."

"I'm sure they would want to know—"

"Did I ask for your opinion?"

Any other man would have been cowed by James McCormick's tone, but Gerald took it in stride.

"No, sir."

"I don't appreciate my chauffeur telling me how to live my life."

All right. That was *it*.

"If I were just a chauffeur, sir, I would agree. But I am your security detail as well, and I would be remiss in my duties if I left you alone while compromised." Gerald pulled out his best commanding voice, planning on the spot, figuring out all the moving parts as they rolled out so he could find a way to make sure the old man was going to be okay.

128

"Excuse me?" The belligerent tone was fading, though McCormick's demeanor was stiff.

"It's a matter of corporate integrity, sir." Thinking on his feet, Gerald decided the best approach was to appeal to the man's sense of pride and his business acumen. "Anterdec needs you. I work for Anterdec. I would hate to have to face the board of directors in the future to explain why I left one of their most valuable assets ill and alone."

"Their *most* valuable asset," McCormick corrected him with another *harumph*.

"Of course."

"Andrew may be CEO now, but I built this company from the ground up. I sacrificed and deferred." He paused, taking in a slow, deep breath. "I gave everything to my company."

"And your results are admirable."

McCormick watched him, eyes narrowing, as he breathed slowly and thoroughly, clearly working on managing whatever physical state made him so pale, so angry.

"Yes. They are."

"And a man of your stature should have someone here to help take care of any matters that might require assistance, like phone calls, rescheduling, errands..."

"That person is you."

"Sir, I have a two p.m. appointment. I have to leave by half past one." He looked at the clock. 11:15. "Should I call Becky?"

"Becky?" McCormick's eyes flew open. He looked like someone shot him in the chest. "Hell, no." Rumor had it the old man had been sleeping with his executive admin for a few years, and Gerald had wondered.

Confirmation comes in the strangest moments.

"Then who?"

While McCormick closed his eyes and refused to answer, Gerald realized he had the answer.

Pam.

When you work for wealthy people long enough, you learn an important lesson: time really is money. Make yourself valuable enough, and you can get away with murder. Being irreplaceable is a form of job security, because for the wealthy, the transition of training someone new to handle their quirks was more painful than almost any employee behavior.

He took a calculated risk and sent a quick text to Pam Warrick. Her daughter Amanda, Andrew McCormick's fiancée, had given him the number a long time ago when he'd been tasked with picking up Pam. Gerald liked her. Quiet, smart, easy to talk to, and humble.

The opposite of what he expected in a friend of James McCormick, but the world had a way of continually surprising Gerald.

So did people.

Bzzz.

Be there in thirty, she typed back.

Gerald's shoulders loosened with relief. He'd rather incur McCormick's wrath at reaching out to Pam without permission than deal with the guilt of knowing he'd been ill and alone.

"Gerald," McCormick said, his voice gaining strength. "Get me home. The Back Bay."

"Can you handle the drive, sir?" Not that driving him to his house in the suburbs would be any easier.

He let out a shaky breath. "I'll manage."

Twenty minutes later, Gerald was parked in front of McCormick's brownstone, a stand-alone building with a private garden. The estate in Weston was for entertainment and show. Most of McCormick's time was spent here, in the five-bedroom, three-bath home with an English courtyard garden maintained by two master gardeners.

Unfortunately, the building involved stairs.

Stairs that loomed large in Gerald's eyes. He could carry the guy easily, but McCormick would never, ever agree to that.

Not, at least, while conscious.

"I'm fine," McCormick protested, as if reading Gerald's mind. "Just winded."

It took a while, but the guy made it into the large front room of the first story and settled into a comfortable leather wingback chair.

Gerald sprang to action. Unable to get ginger beer in time, he resorted to making lemon tea for James McCormick, delivering it just as the front buzzer rang.

Busted.

And yet, McCormick just looked at him and said, "Get the door."

He did.

Pam Warrick stood there, purse on her arm, tiny teacup Chihuahua named Spritzy peeking his head out.

"Ma'am."

"Call me Pam, Gerald."

"Hello, Pam. He doesn't know I texted you," Gerald admitted in a soft voice.

"He texted me three minutes after you did, Gerald. Your secret is safe."

Without meaning to, he smiled.

"You look so different when you grin!" Pam exclaimed, walking with great care as she made her way to McCormick's living room. Gerald was surprised. She seemed to know her way around.

"Pam? Is that you?"

At the sound of McCormick's voice, Spritzy leaped from the purse on Pam's arm and scampered across the marble floor, onto the Persian rug, and clambered up McCormick's leg.

"There you are," he muttered. "Best medicine any man could have." Cracking one eye open, James McCormick looked at Pam.

"You should have texted me sooner, James," she chided, walking to him, planting a sweet kiss on the crown of his ash-colored head.

"I'm fine. I just needed some doggie love."

Pam quirked an eyebrow at Gerald.

Who shook his head.

She nodded. Message received.

"What went wrong?"

"Stupid doctors," McCormick grumbled. "Fools. Something about my labs. *Blah blah blah* kidney problem, so they halted treatment. Said I could try again in a few weeks." He *harumphed* again, sounding like a walrus with strep throat.

"But the cancer?"

"It's holding steady. No growth. This is just maintenance." He waved a lazy hand.

The audible sound of relief from Pam made Gerald pay more attention to the dynamic between the two of them. People-watching wasn't a habit.

It was a job requirement.

"Then what's wrong?"

"Nausea," James McCormick finally confessed. "And fatigue. You know how tiring running a Fortune 500 company can be."

Pam gave him a look Gerald couldn't discern. "The doctors gave you something for the nausea, I assume."

"Yes. Didn't help."

"That I understand. Medicines that don't work." Gerald knew that Pam suffered from fibromyalgia. He'd helped her to walk up her porch stairs before.

132

"I wish the damn doctors could find a way to make this go away."

Pam's eyes darted to Gerald, then James. She leaned over and whispered in the old man's ear.

He jerked so quickly that Spritzy leaped off his lap and skittered to the ground, nervous.

"Pamela! I cannot believe you would suggest such a thing."

Her cheeks pinked.

Gerald started to slowly move toward the kitchen. Apparently, he'd underestimated their relationship. He had no desire to be around when they went to the bedroom and—

"You mean," James McCormick asked stiffly, not making eye contact with Pam, "you want me to inhale *The Reefer*?"

James McCormick's expression made it clear that Pam might as well have just asked him to vote for Bernie Sanders.

If the man had been wearing a set of pearls, he'd be clutching them.

And Gerald was off. *Way* off.

Thank God.

"Haven't you—haven't you ever tried it, James?" Pam asked.

He didn't answer the question. "If I want to escape, a bottle of whisky does the job."

"Marijuana is considerably superior to alcohol, James, as a nausea treatment," Pam began. She pulled her flowery-print skirt under her knees and sat on the couch across from him, smiling. "The endocannabinoid system is a—"

"It's for *hippies*," McCormick shot back.

"Then call me a hippie," Pam said dryly.

McCormick reeled back with shock, then groaned, touching his forehead as if in pain. "You? *You're* a pothead?"

Pam's giggle was infectious. Gerald had to force himself not to react.

"I'm a human being with a painful medical condition, and once in a while, I use an ancient herb prized for its pain relief and anti-nausea properties to get some relief."

"Pam, you are rationalizing."

"And you're stalling." She picked up her phone and tapped. "I have a medical marijuana card, but there aren't any dispensaries in the state yet. I have a friend who can deliver some."

"You're going to send a drug dealer here? To my home? Absolutely not!"

"She isn't a drug dealer. She just dabbles."

"I know you think that what you're doing is helpful," James said, wincing. "But—" A fine sheen of sweat broke out on his forehead.

"I texted her before I even came, James. She's a few minutes away."

"I can't believe this," he gasped. "I'm *fine*."

"You are a stubborn mule. *Fine* is the last word I would use to describe you."

"When did you become such a nag? You sound like my wife." But his voice was filled with mirth. Amusement. A sense of being pleased that someone was doting on him.

Pam's eyes widened at his words. "Someone needs to remind you that you matter."

"Of course I matter!"

"Then let people help you."

"Breaking federal law is not my idea of help, Pam."

Ding!

The doorbell.

Without being asked, Gerald rose and went to the door, finding an all-too-familiar face peeking through the beveled glass.

"Mrs. Jacoby," he said as she entered the house head first, craning her neck to take in James McCormick's mini-mansion.

She let out a low whistle.

"I've never seen this place. Only his home in Weston. The other half lives like this in downtown Boston, huh?" She gave Gerald a hug. He wasn't a hugger, but duty called. Marie Jacoby was one of the more fascinating people he worked with. She was a walking contradiction. Smart but ditzy. Demanding but deferential. Cunning but obvious.

In spite of all that, he liked her.

But he wasn't sure why.

"I wonder what this place is worth," she whispered.

"I assume you're here to meet with Mr. McCormick," he said, cutting her off.

"Yes. I have his—" She cleared her throat and wiggled her eyebrows.

He decided to have some fun.

"His what?"

"His medicine."

"The doctor didn't prescribe any," Gerald shot back.

"Dr. MJ certainly did."

"Dr. MJ?"

"You know. Dr. Feelgood."

Gerald wasn't about to point out that she was misappropriating that music culture reference.

"What kind of doctor is this Dr. Feelgood?"

"The kind that makes you feel all right."

He closed his eyes and groaned. When he opened them, she was grinning at him.

"Are you single, Gerald? Because I have a daughter."

"You have three, ma'am."

135

"One is married!"

"Yes, ma'am. Well aware."

"But two aren't."

He stayed silent.

She frowned. "Are you gay?"

"No."

"Available?"

He hesitated just long enough to make her perk up.

"Oooo, you have a wife? Girlfriend?"

"No." He had to answer honestly.

"Then—"

"Marie!" Pam called from the other room. Spritzy jangled across the marble floor, dog tags making a rhythm. He reached Marie, licked her ankle, and looked up expectantly.

Pick me up, that little dog face said.

Marie looked at her shoes, laces riding up the top of her foot.

"Thank God you're not Chuckles," she muttered as she walked into the living room, carrying the dog. Pam waved.

James McCormick groaned.

"Her? *She* is your drug dealer? This just went from immoral to unbelievable." Spritzy flung himself out of Marie's arms into James McCormick's lap.

"That's me!" Marie chirped.

"Is this a sting operation?" He looked at Gerald. "You are my security team. Why aren't you helping here? They're cajoling me into imbibing illegal substances!"

"Would you like me to throw them out?"

Spritzy began licking James' face.

"The dog is clearly assaulting you," Pam added dryly.

136

Marie squinted at James. "What century were you born in? C'mon, James. It's a little weed. We're not asking you to eat a live goat on television."

"But marijuana is illegal!" He pronounced the word with a harsh H sound.

"So is insider trading," Marie shot back.

He paled.

"If it'll make you feel better, let's do a little doobie. Can't hurt," Marie cajoled. She and Pam shared a conspirators' look. She reached into her purse and pulled out a small baggie. "Here's the good stuff. You ready to roll?"

"Roll?"

A small packet appeared in her hand. "Roll. Rolling papers. Get it?"

"This is not happening in my home," James groaned.

"You've never, ever smoked marijuana?" Marie asked, giving him a look that said, *I know otherwise.*

He closed his eyes.

"Not in thirty-plus years."

"You mean not since you got high with me in my loft."

He snorted. "Loft? You call a rat-infested warehouse I owned your *loft*?" Gerald knew the two had dated decades ago, but this was new information.

"Yes."

"You are delusional."

"Not yet, but three hits and I will be."

"What does your husband think about this? He lets you do illegal recreational drugs with wanton abandon?"

Marie halted mid-roll. "Let? Did you just say *let*?" She cackled, deeply amused. "First of all, no man needs to *let* me do anything." She licked the edge of the paper, continuing to speak. "And second, who do you think gave me the rolling papers?"

Gerald just watched. It was his job. Some days were boring.

And then there were days like this.

He'd done his fair share of toking, so he wasn't judging. Marie rolled a fattie and pulled out a hot-pink lighter. The *snick* of the flint making the flame took him back to a time when a few hits off a bowl were the only solace he and his fellow soldiers had.

It wasn't his go-to for escape, though.

Sculpting was.

His hands itched to get into the studio, back at home, and just throw himself into a sensory world where he made his way through curve and angle, bump and swell, through the tenuous connection between mind's eye and tactile pressure.

Instead, he busied himself by walking into the kitchen and starting a pot of coffee. While James McCormick didn't have the stomach for it, he knew the two women loved their cup o' joe.

"I know how to take a toke of the devil's weed, Marie," he heard McCormick bluster, followed by the natter-chatter of Marie prattling on about proper inhalation technique.

"It's about the ratio of THC to CBD," Pam said. "It needs to be right."

Whoooooo.

The unmistakable sound of a deep inhale through bud, stems, leaves and seeds filled the air.

And then a strong scent followed. But it was odd. Huh. Must be skunk weed.

As the coffee gurgled, Gerald checked the time. 12:40 p.m. He had to leave by 1:30 to get to his two o'clock appointment at Suzanne's law firm.

Suzanne.

Inheritance.

Artifact. Harrison Kulli. The words took shape in his mind, gaining texture and topology, form and spirit. He integrated with the shape, becoming an extension of whatever he touched, finding freedom in sculpture.

Only through making the shape of something he created in the connection between mind and eye could he find his own boundaries.

The coffee nearly finished, the machine's noise was diminishing, though Gerald had been able to hear each toke they'd taken. He poured coffee into a thermal carafe, arranged cups on a tray, pulled cream from the refrigerator and grabbed a sugar bowl and spoons.

"Are there any downsides to huffing the wacky tobbacky?" James asked after exhaling his third hit, just as Gerald walked in with the coffee.

Pam frowned. "Other than short-term memory issues, the only negative research I'm aware of involves erectile dysfunction." She smiled at him and insisted on pouring.

James McCormick's eyes bugged out of his head.

"Pam," he gasped. "You could have mentioned that *before* I inhaled!" He looked down at his crotch, worried.

"What kind of music do you have on your stereo, James?" Marie asked, poking around the large floor-to-ceiling oak cabinets.

"The good kind." Gerald could sense a shift in his tone, a lessening of tension. Pam looked at McCormick, her hand on Spritzy's head, her eyes evaluative.

Marie pressed a button.

The Carpenters came on. The opening chords to the song "Just Like Me" filled the room.

"EWWWWWWW," Pam and Marie called out in unison.

Marie pushed a button.

Barry Manilow's "Can't Smile Without You" started.

Pam and Marie turned on the old man, both of them frowning.

"Seriously, James?" Pam asked, as if he'd personally offended her.

"What?" he asked groggily, opening his eyes slowly. "Pammy, you look good when you're angry." He licked his palm and reached for Spirtzy, slicking back a shock of hair that stuck up.

"Please tell me you have some kind of music other than easy listening," Marie moaned.

Pam pressed a button on the complex stereo. It looked like the control panel for a 747. Gerald hadn't seen a stereo set-up like that since he'd visited a Vietnam vet's house for a BBQ and gotten a lecture on all the electronics he'd brought back from Japan in 1973.

"So help me God, if 'Girl from Ipanema' comes on, I'll—"

It did.

"You'll *what*, Pam?" Marie asked.

Pam just laughed.

Rummaging through vinyl album after vinyl album in a long, thick row that constituted James McCormick's record collection, Marie squealed with horror until she perked up, clutching a familiar release.

Pink Floyd's "The Wall."

"Where did you unearth that?" James growled, opening only one eye.

"Someone has good music taste," Marie declared. "It's not you!"

"Andrew?" Pam wondered aloud.

"Elena," James said.

Pam went quiet. Gerald watched her, fascinated.

"She liked classic rock?"

"Where do you think Andrew and Terry get it? She used to take Terry to concerts when he was younger."

"I always thought Elena was an uptight blue blood," Marie said.

"She was. And she enjoyed Led Zeppelin, Yes, and all those other crazy performers."

"Good for her," Pam said softly. "I wish I could have met her."

"I wish I could have had more years with her," James confessed.

The opening notes of "Comfortably Numb" filled James McCormick's living room.

"This pop music crap," McCormick said, though a smile twitched at the corner of his lips.

"James," Marie asked slyly, "how are you feeling now?"

"Goooood."

"Excellent." She sidled in next to him. Gerald heard her whisper, "You know, we're good friends. And as your friend, I'd like to talk to you about that $700,000 my husband gave back to your casino. I think it's all just a big misunderstanding." She patted his hand.

McCormick's eyes flew wide open and he glowered.

"Not so comfortably numb now. You're harshing on my groove, Marie."

She shrugged, as if to say it couldn't hurt to *try*.

"Gerald, would you make some Rice Krispie Treats for us?" Marie asked sweetly, eyes round like buckeyes, changing the topic masterfully.

"With Cheetos," Pam added.

"And anchovies," James insisted.

Gerald nodded, retreating to the kitchen, relieved to be out of sight where he could laugh and react to the absurdities.

As he checked the cupboards for supplies, the front door opened.

On high alert, he put his hand on the butt of his gun in the holster beneath his jacket.

"Hello?"

That voice was unmistakable.

Terry McCormick.

Gerald stood down.

"What happened? Is Dad okay?"

That was Andrew McCormick.

"Oh, man!" James McCormick groaned. "Who invited them?"

Declan appeared behind Andrew. Terry wore a paint-stained Rush t-shirt, while the other two brothers were in fine cashmere suits, one on either side of Terry, like Jackson Pollock and his bankers.

Terry glanced at Declan and Andrew, shrugged, and sat down on the couch, reaching for the joint.

"Terry!" Andrew bellowed. Gerald watched him carefully. The guy wasn't horrified.

He was *jealous*.

Terry just shrugged. He took a long hit off the fattie and his eyes flew open as he hacked up half a lung.

"Amateur," James muttered.

Terry barked out a coughing laugh. "This isn't pot!"

"What?" Andrew and Declan snapped in unison, Declan's emotions moving swiftly across his face, from stunned shock to suppressed amusement.

Terry bent over, his head between his knees, shoulders shaking with uncontrolled laughter. "This—" he wheezed, "isn't pot. It's *not* marijuana." He looked up, eyes bloodshot from crying, not from THC, and announced to Pam, James and Marie, "You're all high on oregano."

"I wondered why I have a sudden craving for garlic bread," James declared. He turned to Gerald. "I'd like you to go to the North End and get me—"

"Oregano?" Marie squeaked. "OREGANO?" She stood, mouth dropping open in outrage. "Agnes told me

142

this was the finest weed her grandson could get his hands on."

"I'll bet it is," Declan said, smothering a smile.

"I gave Agnes six free yoga classes for that dime bag!"

Never barter with Agnes, Gerald thought.

"Maybe it's homeopathic marijuana," Terry choked out, which only made Marie turn red with fury.

"You mean we're not really high?" Pam asked.

"No," Terry said. Gerald watched Declan, who leaned against the arm of his father's wingback chair, one hand in his suit pants pocket, the other thumbing through messages on his phone.

"That explains it, then," Marie announced. "I'm normally horny as can be when I'm high, and I'm dead below the waist right now."

Without a single word, as smooth as Gene Kelly in an old 1940s musical movie, Declan spun around on one shoe and left the room, the back of his head visibly shaking to and fro, a loud sigh echoing through the foyer. The click of the front door snapping shut came soon after.

Nothing like hearing your mother-in-law announce *that*.

"Me, too!" Pam announced.

Andrew made a strange retching sound and suddenly became deeply fascinated with a stray string on his shirt cuff.

Ding! Doorbell.

"I'll get it!" Andrew announced, practically shoving Gerald aside in his hurry to escape the room. Gerald folded his hands at the waist and waited, trying not to react to the unfolding scene before him.

And then in walked the last person he ever expected to see standing in James McCormick's Back Bay home.

"Suzanne?" he rasped, her heels click-clacking on the marble floor. Spritzy jumped out of James' arms and ran over to Suzanne, sniffing her ankles.

Too bad Gerald couldn't display that kind of public enthusiasm.

Andrew walked past her, poured himself a coffee, and settled in on the couch next to Pam, crossing his legs, face filled with a combination of disruptive anger and marvel.

"Someone found Mom's old album collection," he said with approval.

"Well, damn!" James' voice boomed through the room, deeper somehow, closer to Terry's bass. The sound was loud enough to make Suzanne flinch slightly, frown, then look at the old man.

"I'm sorry, James. I had no idea it was oregano," Marie said again, clearly flummoxed.

Oregano? Suzanne mouthed to Gerald.

Why are you here? he mouthed back.

James' face screwed up in contemplation. Everyone looked at him, waiting.

"If that had been real reefer, I might have had my first threesome!" he exclaimed, looking directly at Gerald. "Does anyone in the room know how to get the real stuff?"

Suzanne's single eyebrow arch said everything and nothing.

"Suzanne?" Terry asked, the surprise on his face evident. "What—it's great to see you, but what are you doing here?"

"James asked for me."

"Is this about our mother's trust fund?"

She gave him a quizzically apologetic smile as her eyes tracked James, who now held the joint aloft and studied it, mumbling, "Are you sure this isn't real?"

144

"I'm afraid," Suzanne said, clearly not, "that I can't talk about why I'm here. But James asked me to visit him in an official capacity."

"I forgot. My apologies, Suzanne. I'm indisposed," James said, waving toward her.

She stared at the joint in his hand. "I see that."

Andrew started laughing. Gerald watched as Terry joined him.

She turned to Gerald. "We have a two o'clock at my office," she said, in earshot of Andrew, who frowned.

"You two know each other?"

"Sort of," said Suzanne.

"Yes," said Gerald.

Terry stopped laughing and watched them.

"James," Suzanne said. "This looks like a bad time for our meeting. Why don't I have my assistant call yours for a reschedule? I can help with Elena's family trust any time."

"Oh," James said, eyes closed, head against the back of the couch. Spritzy was on his chest. "This isn't about the family trust."

"Then what?"

"It's about buying that secret artifact Harold Hopewell's been hiding from the world all these years."

CHAPTER TEN

Suzanne sat at the head of the enormous oval conference table, a relic of its own from the nineteenth century that Norm Phelps' grandfather had imported from the Ukraine when he'd founded Phelps, Miller in 1911. Both the Phelps and the Miller families still had descendants in partner roles, all male. She was the second woman to make partner, and relished every second of being on top.

Her eyes darted to Gerald.

She would love to be on top of *him*.

The last hour had been a study in chaos. As she shuffled folders and managed the never-ending flow of documents Letitia and Margaret provided, she ran through the facts as she knew them.

James McCormick was interested in buying the relic.

He was not the same anonymous donor Harrison Kulli represented.

More people knew about the relic than previously recognized.

The relic was increasingly endangered as the circle of knowledge widened. The more people who knew about it, the more likely it was to be stolen or desecrated.

And yet, exposing its existence to official institutions wouldn't necessarily help.

"Change of plans," Norm said, walking into the room with that penguin-like gait he had. He introduced himself to Gerald, looked at Suzanne, and said, "Turns out the MFA archaeologist has no knowledge of the item. We had to be careful." He reached down for a leather bag that looked like it contained a tiny bowling ball.

Lifted it like it weighed a ton.

"Here it is. Your inheritance," he said to Gerald, who looked appropriately shocked. Glancing at the door, twisting in his seat to do a 180-degree spin, he became increasingly angry.

"No armed guard? No security of any kind? Are you crazy? That thing's worth eight figures—" As he cut off his own words, Gerald's face paled, eyes going wide like moons.

Suzanne felt sorry for him.

"We do not need security for an item no one's heard of," Phelps insisted, pinching the bridge of his nose. "And there's a team of six guys out in the hall. Don't worry."

"James McCormick has heard of it. Worse— Harrison Kulli sure as *hell* has. That guy would smother his own grandmother for a scratch lottery ticket," Gerald said with a grunt of disgust.

Suzanne nodded.

Phelps simmered.

"Take a careful look. Is this the relic you recall?" Phelps slid the bag across the table to Gerald, who unzipped it. The sound of the ancient brass zipper opening was like the gates to hell creaking on their hinges.

She held her breath.

Gerald's face went remarkably blank.

And that's when she realized just how serious this really was. When the man wiped all emotion from his body, it was time to set your own alert scale on high.

"Yes," he said simply.

"You never told me," she blurted out, the words completely unexpected.

His eyes met hers.

"There's a lot I've never told you."

"Clearly."

Phelps cleared his throat. "I'll leave you two to figure this all out. Discretion is paramount."

"Of course," Suzanne said, not looking away from Gerald.

He stared, unblinking, at the open bag.

"Harold Hopewell. Never met the guy. I've heard of him. Hell, everyone has. Why this? Why *me*? And why does James McCormick want the relic?" Gerald's words came out like an assault weapon being fired.

"You told him about it," Suzanne said, her voice low.

"No, I didn't," he said gruffly. "You think I went back to work and started bragging?"

The Gerald she knew would have kept his mouth shut.

Phelps stopped in the doorway, his back still to them. "I can answer that," he said quietly, turning around and almost closing the door behind him. He held onto the doorknob like a tether.

"Why?" Suzanne asked.

"Because wealthy, self-made men like to acquire. It's not about the money. Not even about the power. They just want to possess something no one else has."

"That's too simple," Suzanne argued.

"Simple or not, it's true. Once James McCormick learned about the relic—however he learned about it— he wanted it. Simple." He exited, leaving Suzanne alone with Gerald.

Who was a robot.

"Say something," she urged.

Reaching into the bag, he pulled out a velvet pouch, making a clear effort to lift the heavy object. The velvet was old, sun-stained and the color of faded rust. As he pulled gently on the drawstring, it snapped, leaving frayed ends.

And then gold. Gold and more gold, in the shape of a fertility goddess birthing a tiny human being.

Suzanne nearly laughed. It looked like a souvenir from a cheesy shop.

It was anything but.

"James McCormick can't tell the difference between marijuana and oregano, but he wants to spend a large fortune on owning this. Why?"

"Doesn't make sense to me either, but that's not my job. My job is to usher you through the inheritance process. Step one's been done. You got the papers. Step two is: do you want to keep it? Sell it? Donate it?"

"I want to hold it."

And he did, for the next two minutes, cradling it, those damn hands of his making love to a pre-Buddhist gold statue that supposedly held the secret to the oldest known civilization in the world.

And damn if Suzanne wasn't a little bit envious.

Of the statue.

"Dinner," he said, eyes flashing as they met hers.

"Dinner?" The clock on the wall read 2:21 p.m.

"Early dinner. Late lunch. Call it what you want." He stood, carefully putting the relic back in the velvet pouch, then in the leather bag, zipping it slowly, like a surgeon making sure the stitches were perfect.

"Go out with me. Talk to me. Spend time with me. Not as a client, but as a friend. I need a friend more than I need a lawyer right now."

"Finally," she said, her voice curt, eyes burning. "You finally make a move. Friend? We both know that's bullshit."

His mouth spread into a smile, but his eyes were so serious.

"I've missed you more than I've realized."

"You should."

"Let me make it up to you."

"You're going to make up ten years?"

"Let me do it in time increments measured by meals out, starting with this one."

"That's a lot of lunches and dinners."

"I have a healthy appetite."

The pull of *yes* was hard to fight. So hard. She looked at his hands, those twitching fingers that couldn't stay still. Restless, always, they needed to make sense of the world through touch.

She knew if she agreed to dinner that they would end up in bed.

She knew that.

And she knew she should fight this. Knew she'd get hurt.

"Yes," she replied.

Because knowing the truth and living your life came into conflict sometimes.

"I know a great place," he said, staring at the leather bag. "A few blocks away, tucked away behind this food court."

He named the same restaurant where she'd just spent lunch two hours ago with Chandler the Puppy.

Her stomach flipped. "I got sick there," she protested.

Without hesitation, he named a great Mexican place in Cambridge.

"Sold," she said with a smile.

They stood there, the sun breaking through the clouds, the view from the conference room one of the city, the streets in the Financial District like wind tunnels. Phelps, Miller was on the fourth floor of her building, so the only view was urban, cold and utilitarian.

Each second that ticked by made anticipation build in her. All these years, she'd been so hurt. Angry. Filled with unspeakable rage.

And now that he was just a man standing in front of her, asking her to be a friend in a time of need, she felt it all recede.

But more than that—she had a chance.

A chance to get answers.

Suzanne wasn't about to put pride before that chance.

She texted Letitia, who brought all six security guards in to take the relic back to Hopewell's place, leaving her and Gerald ready to move on to the next phase of the day.

As they walked out of the building, Gerald in his uniform of black pants, black blazer, and white business shirt open at the neck, she watched his blank emotional state peel away as if sandblasted.

"Jesus," he said, wiping his mouth with his hand. "Fifty million. Two billionaires are offering fifty million for that."

"You're wealthy." She snapped her fingers. "Just like that."

"I'd trade it all for—"

A box truck in front of them laid on the horn, hard and long, before he could say the next word.

The moment was lost.

He was about to say *you*.

She was sure.

And if he would trade it all for her, why wouldn't he talk to her for ten years?

Walking paradox. The man was a walking paradox.

He hailed a cab with fluency and command. The ride across the river to Cambridge was quiet. Each lost in their own thoughts, both buzzed constantly by texts for various work issues, they didn't talk.

At all.

Suzanne's knee brushed against him as the driver took a right turn too tightly. Every bit of concentration in her body focused on the spot where they touched.

He looked at her knee. She looked at him.

They said nothing.

Deposited in front of the Mexican place, she and Gerald found their way inside. Once seated, she decided to go for the jugular.

"Ten years. Explain."

"You could wait until they at least bring the chips and salsa, Suz. A man needs a little sustenance before being raked over the coals."

"I could. But I'm not."

He laughed. "You deserve the whole story." The smile faded from his face.

"I deserve more than that."

"Yes," he said softly. "You do. And this time, I'll be honorable. Ask away."

"I just did. Why did you leave?"

The struggle played out on his face. He opened his mouth to answer.

The server appeared with tortilla chips and salsa.

"Saved," he joked.

She gave him a hard stare. Every molecule of her body was on fire. She felt all the feelings all at once, as if time folded into every emotion across every second in this scene. Pushing her hair off her shoulders, she watched him. A sense of redemption filled her.

Did he feel a glimmer of atonement? That kiss last night said more than *I'm sorry*.

What would he actually *say*?

"Why did you leave?" she persisted.

"Because I was out of my mind."

She picked up her purse and started to stand. He lunged, his hand gripping her wrist in a vise.

"Don't go."

"Then don't lie."

"Not lying. Starting to explain. Give me a chance here, Suz. This isn't easy."

"You think it is for me?" Her heart relocated to her wrist.

"No." He let go, his eyes desperate, animal-like in the way they worked the room. Alighting on her, he stared at her with so much heat and lust she almost burst into flames. "But now that you're here, in front of me, and that line's been crossed, I can't go back. That doesn't mean I know what I'm doing."

"The Gerald Wright I knew ten years ago always knew what he was doing."

"I'm not that man anymore. Probably never was."

She sat down, gravity dragging her, the shock of his words leaving her boneless.

"I don't believe that."

"Believe whatever you want. Maybe after I explain, you'll see it my way." He took a sip of water. The skin at the hollow of his neck was bright red, a telltale sign of stress in him.

"Okay." She reached for a tortilla chip just to do something with her hands. "Explain."

"After the suicide bomber, I couldn't think." No need for clarity on this topic; Suzanne knew exactly who and what he was talking about. Three months before he dumped her, Gerald's team had come across a suicide bomber, a guy wearing a vest of explosives. The team of five American soldiers had found him standing in the market. A sharp-eyed kid from Indiana, just off the plane, spotted the guy.

Carrying his toddler son in his arms, screaming about glory.

Split second decisions come with costs.

154

Gerald's team had tried to find a way to disarm the guy and separate the child from him. The vest had detonated just as another child of about five or so had flung himself in the bomber's arms.

It had ended badly.

"You did everything—"

Gerald's palm shot up.

"This isn't about that. It's about what happened after."

"I remember."

"You don't, Suz. You really don't."

Her throat tightened, a lump poking her, making tears push against her eyelids. "Then tell me. Please."

"I am." He paused. "It takes time."

"We've had ten years."

"Might not be long enough." The stark look he gave her was heartbreaking.

"I won't push."

He smiled halfway. "You are constitutionally incapable of not pushing."

"Is that why you broke up with me the way you did? Because you knew I'd push."

Slowly, achingly, he looked up from the table, meeting her eyes.

"Yes."

"Damn it."

"I knew if I saw you I couldn't leave. That I'd drag you down."

"Why? Why did you leave?"

"Because I was out of my mind, Suz. I ended up in long-term therapy back home. Took two years for the nightmares to stop."

"I would have been there with you, through it all."

"I know you would have. That's why I had to let you go."

"Don't play this macho bullshit with me, Gerald. You're better than this. And I damn well know I am. Don't feed me lines like this."

"I'm not. I'm telling the truth."

"The whole truth?"

His face flickered with admiration and disgust, a strange combination that Suzanne found oddly titillating.

"It must suck to live life with that perfect bullshit detector. What a curse."

He might as well have slapped her and caressed her at the same time. This was what she missed the most. A man who could slip into shorthand with her, who understood her at a fundamentally different level than the rest of the world. The rarity of that kind of connection made her watch him, breathing through a decade of scar tissue, and realize that the past didn't matter.

Truly.

How much longer was she going to deprive herself of being this well understood? Her anger was a shield against the injustice of what Gerald had done to her, but it was also a shell she used to justify hiding from the world. Three years of law school, seven years of hundred-hour weeks left her with virtually nothing to give to any sector of her life.

Least of all her heart.

She liked it that way.

Until now.

"It's a gift."

He snorted. "It's a gift when it helps you. I don't think it's helping you right now."

Damn it.

He did it again.

"How do you do that?"

"Do what?"

156

"Know me so well? Even after all these years you just...do."

"It's a gift." He didn't smirk as he threw her own words back at her.

"It really is."

She started to breathe as slowly as possible as her heart crawled into her throat, her stomach curling inward, her thighs tightening. He could just look at her and make this happen. He could give her a raw, unafraid appraisal and rip out the deep roots of discontent that had grown there in his absence.

She grabbed a tortilla chip and shoveled it in her mouth, the crunching a welcome static, breaking up the silence in her mind.

Gerald did that.

He quieted her, the internal voice silenced, the eerie echo leaving room for true emotion to seep in.

For him to walk back in.

"That's it? You had PTSD like every other soldier—including me—and you left because of that?"

"Basically."

"Basically doesn't cut it."

"I came home and spent nearly two months in a psych ward, Suz. That email was a gesture of mercy. Took me two years to get out of my own head and start living again."

"I'm sorry."

"I don't need your pity."

"I'm not offering it. The fact that you don't know the difference between pity and empathy is really sad."

He gagged on his water.

"Your walking out on me was the single worst thing that ever happened to me, Gerald. Ever."

Eyes watering, he tried to recover and speak, his throat in spasms. "I'm sure that's not true, Suz. You saw some roadside bombings that—"

"Don't you dare—you, of all people—try to tell me my own internal state, Gerald. You don't get to invalidate me. You don't get to rank my emotional devastation." Her voice was deadly calm. "You never had permission to do so, and you certainly don't have it now."

Pain flashed in his eyes. "You're right. Forgive me."

Forgive me.

Could she? Could she ever? As the waiter delivered a platter of enchiladas and quesadillas and they busied themselves, grateful for the break, she wondered. Could she ever forgive him? Or herself? Because if the answer was no, she was wasting time.

Hers and his.

"I've imagined this moment so many times," she confessed. Why not? What did she have to lose. Worst case, her anger. It might be nice to set down that burden for good and stop letting it weight her down. "And not once did I think that when I explained how hurt I was by your leaving, you'd compare it to a roadside bombing and say that having the love of my life break my heart by email and then disappear wasn't as bad."

He closed his eyes and winced.

"And yet, every part of me wants to throw myself at you and be kissed like last night. I want to pour out my heart and pick that fine mind of yours. I want to watch you sculpt, observe how you move through the world with your body, taking in parts of life I only see at surface depth. So here I am, hating you and left with the echo of loving you so deeply, and for so long, that I think I held on to the anger because it was all I had left of you."

With that, she grabbed a triangle of quesadilla, dipped it in sour cream, and took a bite.

Gerald's eyes tightened, narrowing so much she could barely see the pupils. He leaned forward, his cuff brushing the tips of the chips in the basket, and whispered, "The biggest mistake of my life was not knowing how to trust you."

She felt the words as they traveled from her brain to her heart, triggering biochemical systems designed to unite emotion with stimulus, biology with communication.

"And sitting here, across this table, watching you tell me how much I hurt you, and yet you still want what we once had, blows my mind. You always did that, Suzanne. And you still do that. Only you."

A part of her knew he was holding back. There was more. Much more.

But another self inside her, one she'd shushed a thousand times, wanted to walk into his arms and be held.

"How have you been?" she asked softly. "How did you heal?"

"How do you know I have?"

"You said you're a different man."

He reached across the table and slid his hand into hers. Didn't ask.

Didn't need to.

"That's really the story? You came home ahead of me, got put in psych, emailed me to break up, and by the time I was stateside, no one knew where you were. What were you doing? What was your life like?"

"I spent two years roaming."

"Homeless?"

"No. Roaming. Walked the Appalachian Trail. The California Coastal Trail. Buckeye Trail. Went all over North America."

"You camped?"

"Sometimes. It's—it's not all clear. There was a gradual unfolding over those years. Peace came in layers. I can't give you a coherent narrative."

159

She squeezed his hand. "But you were safe."

"Yeah. Mostly, people were afraid of me."

She took him in. If you never saw him smile, and didn't know how he was under the surface, Gerald was a scary-looking wall of muscle.

"And then I came to Boston. Did some work in a gym. Met my friend, Vince. He kicked my ass and told me to use my background for good. Got in with a security agency and the McCormicks hired me."

"You like it?"

"I'm good at it."

"That's not the question I asked."

"Yeah. I do. I don't think about it much. It's easier to keep moving and not think. That's how I spend most of my time."

"You still like to touch everything?"

"Is your name 'everything'?"

They both laughed.

"Sorry," he said, having the decency to look sheepish. "I think Andrew McCormick's rubbed off on me."

"Is that a work duty?"

"What?"

"Letting him rub—"

He groaned.

She reached for a quesadilla with her free hand, dipped it in sour cream, and watched him do the same.

They never let go of each other's hands.

"Tell me the story about the relic," she blurted out, needing clarity.

He groaned and rolled his eyes. "It's such a stupid story."

The look she gave him said he had no choice but to talk.

Sighing, he conceded and said, "One of those freak moments in the field. A bombed out cave. We were checking for survivors and my hand brushed against this broken wooden box. Kulli saw it, too."

"What?"

"Right. I palmed the relic and shoved it in my pocket before he could see it. He grabbed the broken box and found some other, smaller artifact in there. Went on about how much he could make on the black market. I kept my mouth shut."

"Wise of you."

"And then he went on for the next few weeks about some damn curse."

"Curse?" Norm Phelps had mentioned a curse when he'd met with her about the case. Norm was about as rational as any human being could be.

So was Gerald.

A creeping sensation took over the back of her neck.

Gerald shook his head, finishing a mouthful of food, then taking a swallow of water. "Yeah, curse. I thought he was full of shit at the time, but now..." A haunted look met her inquiring gaze. "Now I wonder."

"You think you're cursed?"

He shrugged.

She smirked.

"And you got the relic into the United States and into Harold Hopewell's private collection...how?"

"The smuggling was easy."

"I can't believe you're throwing these words around so easily. Smuggling an ancient artifact, Gerald! You! You wouldn't jaywalk when I knew you," she joked.

"Kulli would have sold it off. I knew the relic had to be – well, anyhow. I covered the relic in modeling clay, made it look like one of my own pieces, and brought it home during a trip home when my mother was sick."

"And that's that? How did Hopewell get it?"

"I have no idea. I found one of my old art teachers, who knew someone at an art and antiquities dealer, and they promised it would go to someone who would preserve it and appreciate it."

"That's it?"

"That's it. I had no idea it went to Hopewell. None."

She let it all sink in.

Kulli and the black market. Gerald violating so many laws. A cursed relic. Harold Hopewell.

And Gerald, holding her hand, looking at her like she was the most precious object in the world.

"Thank you," he said after some time, both of them having abandoned their half-eaten plates, a shot of tequila for him, a pineapple cosmo mostly drained in front of her. They'd let go of each other's hands and sat now, contemplating the past few hours, finding them wanting.

"For what?"

"For being willing to see me. To come to this late lunch."

"I didn't have a choice. You're my client."

"You always have a choice." He reached for her again, and this time, the implication was clear.

Choose him.

Choose now.

"What am I choosing, Gerald? What is this? Because I'm not going to sleep with you and go back to pretending this didn't happen."

"I'm not asking that of you."

"Then what?"

"I don't know."

"You really have changed. Cocky Gerald would never admit to his inadequacies."

"I said nothing about being inadequate. I said I didn't know. Big difference."

"True. What don't you know?"

"Where I stand. I left you." He shrugged.

162

Suzanne fought the urge to pull her hand away.

"I dumped you. I wasn't thinking rationally. The sad part is that I was so sure that my logic was impeccable. Leaving you meant I would make you avoid the pain of being with me. Forcing you not to be around me made sense. If you weren't near me, you couldn't be in my sphere of influence. I was rescuing you from me." His eyes turned down at the corners.

"Do you ever grow out your hair?" The question poured out of her, subconscious obviously fixated on his head.

He peered at her. "What an odd question."

"I know. I know it is."

"Sometimes. Not in a long while. I grew it out for those first two years home, though."

"Why?"

"I needed to be anyone but me."

"You're you no matter what your hair looks like."

He gave a self-effacing shrug that was so vulnerable she almost cried.

"It's easier to manage when I shave it."

"Would you grow it out for me?"

"Why?"

"So I can see the you I wasn't there to see?"

"I'm not that guy anymore."

"You are, though, Gerald." She leaned into him, her arm pressing against his, the scent of his soap so familiar. When they'd had rare civilian time together, he'd used a soap-aftershave combo that was distinctive. She'd smelled it for years after coming home, bracing herself for disappointment when the odor turned out not to be real.

She'd been chasing something that wasn't there.

Someone.

"Have you had a serious relationship?" he asked, giving her a look that said if she could ask unexpected

163

questions about his appearance, he could up the ante. "Been married?" His voice went gruff on that one.

"Yes and no."

He winced. "Right." She felt his hand go dead in hers.

"Hey. You asked."

"I did. And I'm glad to hear it."

"Glad?"

"Glad you moved on."

"I never really did, though. I just thought I did."

"What are we doing, Suz? Catching up on old times?"

"I don't know. We're talking in circles."

He stood, pulled out his wallet, and put money on the table. "Let's *walk* in circles, then. I have to get out of here."

She stood, following him out, waving at the server.

His arm went around her waist nice and easy, as if it belonged there, as if a decade hadn't passed.

"You really haven't aged."

"Three years of law school and seven years to make partner took years off my life, Gerald. I have under-eye circles that could double as football player smudges."

"No. You're radiant. You're sharper than ever and you carry yourself with more confidence. It's like you became more of the Suzanne I knew." When he smiled, his whole face changed. Melting into that grin would be so easy.

She patted her hip. "A little more."

"Not that." His hand covered hers, pinning her palm against the slope of her rounded hip, down to her ass. "You're more attractive than when I last saw you. Some women lose their shine over time. Your flame just burns brighter."

And with that, they stopped, the kiss a quiet agreement.

Could the past be just the past? She sank into the kiss, wanting to taste his regret, wanting to feel his atonement, needing him to know her pain. Moving beyond these lost ten years meant doing more than acknowledging the wrongs.

They had to make certain not to make the same mistakes again.

They had to be different people this time.

Yet *she* hadn't fundamentally changed.

As his tongue parted her lips, she tightened her grip on his arm, toe-to-toe with him, his hands like bands of steel around her waist, his chest warm against hers. They were right in the middle of the sidewalk, the first hint of autumn chill soaking into her bones, yet she basked in his warmth.

He was here, his mouth against hers, his graceful hands kneading her spine, fingers tracing up as if memorizing. She wondered if he'd sculpted her. Were there statues of the Suzanne she'd been ten years ago? The thought wasn't preposterous; he'd done stunning sculptures of her, tiny statues he kept in his pocket, the clay hard-baked from the heat in Afghanistan, the tokens emotionally stirring for her.

In his wholly unique way, Gerald viewed her body as a lens through which he saw the world, and his hands recreated a permanent talisman of that vantage point. How could she resist?

His body language was so clear, the eagerness making her heart quicken, the hunger to touch stronger than the need for decency. He broke the kiss first with a breathless hitch, then blinked, breathing hard.

"Come back to my place," they said at the same time, with the same weight of a decade pulling their words down, into a register where desire had waited to be unleashed.

"You choose," he insisted, deferring to her in an unnatural way. "It's only fair."

"How is that fair?" she challenged.

"Because I never gave you a choice ten years ago."

She didn't argue, because really, why?

"My place, then," she said, pulling his hand toward the T. "I want you to meet someone."

* * *

"Gerald, meet Smoochy. Smoochy, this is Gerald," Suzanne said as she pulled her keys out of the lock, the half-opened front door to her condo letting the hot air from the non-air-conditioned hall into her living room.

"You have a dog? *You? You* hate dogs!" Gerald said, his rumbling laughter making his chest shake as the little white puffball sniffed his feet, making him step back and sit down on Suzanne's couch.

"I do not!" She handed him a beer.

"You did when I knew you. Said we could never have one," he argued. The little bichon frise climbed into his lap, settled down with her chin on his thigh, and closed her eyes.

"She likes you," Suzanne noted with a smile. "Smoochy doesn't like everyone."

"She has good taste. What made you get a dog?"

"I needed a wingman."

He was taking a swig of the beer when her words sank in. He damn near choked.

"And I guess I wanted somebody to be here when I got home. I don't know. I hit the seven-year mark at work and was made partner. My hours lightened slightly."

"You were lonely."

"I was lonely. Yes."

166

"I keep fighting the urge to apologize. How about I tattoo *I'm sorry* on my ass?" From another man, that would sound sarcastic.

But she could tell he meant it sincerely.

"That would be fun. You'd moon me constantly."

He grinned.

"My loneliness is funny?" Her tone made it clear she was inquiring about his grin.

He shook his head. "No."

She didn't pry.

"Your loneliness makes me wish I had more clarity back then." He patted Smoochy's head. "But this old girl seems to be a good companion. Did you get her as a puppy?"

"Actually, she's a rescue. Had her for less than a year. Her owner had to go into a nursing home."

The look he gave her was touching. "That's really nice of you. To rescue her."

"You know what they say. Not sure who rescued whom."

Smoochy sighed again, her body going limp against Gerald.

"I'll leave you two alone for your intimate moment," Suzanne said with a laugh. "I think *someone* has established herself as the alpha female here."

"My lap's big enough for two," he said, patting his free thigh.

Skin shouldn't warm so quickly, and not from just a few words, a look, a gesture.

But it did.

Her pulse faded, receding, taking with it the steady beat that helped her to know where his body ended and the air began. He met her gaze and they stared. It wasn't that she was uncertain. She wanted him. He wanted her.

What held them back?

167

Civilian life had never been part of them. Suzanne and Gerald had known each other for two years, with snippets back home. A trip to meet his mom and dad. A trip back home when his dad had died of a sudden stroke. Their visit to see her mom in Minnesota. Snatches of time out of war zones.

He'd never seen her apartment, nor she his.

Because they hadn't had one.

"This is so strange," he said.

She was relieved he took the lead. She sat down next to him.

"I know." A thousand questions radiated from her, heat seeking his body, drawing him in.

"You're not in a uniform. I'm not in a uniform. And I'm sitting on your couch in your very nice condo in a great Charlestown neighborhood with your dog drooling on my leg."

"It's surreal."

His voice went rough with emotion. "It's everything I've wanted for years, Suz."

He leaned in, kissing her softly. Smoochy stirred, sat up, and toddled off, jumping off a very distracted Gerald's lap.

"Let's take this," she said, breathless between kisses, "one step at a time."

"Define 'step.'"

"Spend the night with me."

"I like that step."

"Make me breakfast in the morning."

"Is that step two?"

"Sure."

"I always respond well to a clearly defined set of procedures."

"How about a map?"

"Even better."

Neither one moved. The offer, once accepted, was almost enough. Acting on it felt so big. So was he, though. As she crawled into his lap, connected to him by their eager mouths, she pulled her skirt up so she could straddle him, his arms wrapping around her waist. The heat of sinking into him, the intimacy of having his body so close, made her mind rest.

Her body took over.

"You taste so good," he murmured between kisses, his hands sliding up her spine in tandem, then moving across her shoulders in synchronized perfection to remove her suit jacket. The shiver she gave came less from the temperature change and more from the delicious feel of how he touched her. With Gerald, a touch wasn't just the stroke of a finger, the brush of a palm, the flick of a tongue, or the thrust into her. Never one to waste movement, he reveled in it, living fully in dimensions she couldn't even see.

He pulled her shirt out from her waistband just as she returned the favor, seeking the raw warmth of his skin. Her hands flattened against his thick shoulders, the connection grounding, her body moving in a slow, involuntary rhythm against him as he kissed her hard.

So hard.

As he cupped her breasts over her bra, her nipples tightened, the ache spinning down in a spiral, tearing through years of pain and craving. Her breath hitched and his kiss became more urgent, his intent clear. It was so good to kiss a man who knew how to hold her just so, who used a feather light touch where she wanted it, and who pressed where a tighter squeeze made a difference.

Gerald had been joyfully unrestrained in bed, hours of pleasure unending, as if there were no events marking time—no final orgasm, no steps in a schematic—but only the undefined fuzzy logic of imperfect art played out in moans and sighs, in the light stroke of a fingertip against responsive flesh, in the wave of tongue against arched hips and the push and pull of love cried out in ecstasy.

In minutes, they would be back in that dimension.

She shivered with anticipation.

"What are we doing?" she whispered, the tone playful, his hands sinking into her long waves.

"Whatever it is, it's been a while," he rasped. "I've missed you. I've missed *this*." His hand left her breast and traveled up, thumb moving from her chest to her chin, her lips closing over his finger with a warm, wet welcome.

"Like riding a bicycle," she whispered, letting him go. "Except no fish."

"What?"

"Nothing." She shut herself up by kissing him, and within seconds, he was the one doing the kissing, her breath quickening, her blood racing through her, moved by the proximity to him. He was here, in her arms, and she was in his. They were together, finally.

Finally.

He pushed up against her, his erection an invitation, wild heat pooling between her legs, the need for climax rising up in her like a plea. She didn't just want the release that came from any orgasm.

Joining with *him*, coming with *him* was what she wanted desperately.

Him.

"Take me to bed," she murmured against his ear. He kissed her neck, letting a low growl fill the back of his throat, her body primed for the sound. Unbuttoning his shirt, she rushed, the hurried ache too keen, too great, to wait one minute more.

She needed him, needed to feel him inside her, over her, to have him everywhere at once so she could remember what it felt like to be wanted so badly, to be

170

understood so thoroughly, to let yourself go with abandon and trust until you obliterated the boundaries between one body and another.

He moved her gently off him and stood.

She reached for him, lacing her fingers through his.

And led him to the one place where they could put the past where it belonged.

And where the future could roll out before them, naked and vulnerable, completely fresh and stunningly real.

Chapter Eleven

"You totally slept with him," Kari said as she pulled Suzanne into a hug, the mixture of Kari's perfume, ground coffee, and delivery truck exhaust combining to make Suzanne hold back a tickling sneeze.

They were in Kari's favorite new coffee shop, a place whose only redeeming quality seemed to be the baristas, all extremely hot men who looked like male models.

"I did," Suzanne admitted. "How can you tell?" It had been three days since Gerald had spent the night in her apartment, and while they'd both had work issues interfere, a steady stream of texts made it clear that their night together had not been an anomaly.

"Because you look like you finally unclenched."

"Hey!"

"You asked."

Ignoring her, Suzanne peered at the coffee menu. An Americano sounded good. Black coffee on an empty stomach was great fuel. Given her ten a.m. meeting with Phelps, she needed all the reinforcements she could muster.

"How's the coffee here?"

Kari was tracking a guy who looked like a lumberjack, minus the beard. Tailored flannel clung to his abs, so tight Suzanne could see the eight-pack under the tartan.

"Who cares?"

"I do!" She started to take out her wallet and approach the counter. Kari put her hand on her wrist.

"I got this."

Reluctantly, Suzanne put away her money. That was code for *This is a mystery shop*.

"They are all so young," Suzanne said, nearly clucking her tongue. When did she turn into one of the church ladies from her small town back home in Minnesota? Years of military life left her with a fine appreciation for the muscled male form. No need to get shameful about it.

"I know." Was Kari licking her lips? "Eye candy."

"You're objectifying them. You claim to be a feminist."

"I can honor the beauty of the male form and still uphold women's rights."

"You're a horndog."

Kari's silence spoke volumes.

One Americano and one mocha frappuccino abomination later, they sat at a long slab of heavily-varnished oak, precariously teetering on tall aluminum stools that were clearly designed by someone with a torso like taffy. Or Gandalf.

Even Suzanne, a relatively tall woman at 5'10", couldn't find balance.

"I think they designed these to be so uncomfortable that you drink your coffee quickly and leave."

"Who would want to do that?" Kari asked, her eyes on one of the workers watering plants, reaching up with a watering can, his shirt pulling out of his waistband and exposing tanned joy in skin form.

"Cut it out! We're here to talk about my sex life for once."

"That's right! You had sex! How was it?"

Suzanne blushed.

"You—you're blushing! Suz, I didn't know you could do that! He unlocked some blood source inside you, like a spell in a paranormal television series. Ian

Somerhalder is about to come walking through the door."

"How romantic. Thinking about Gerald made me blush."

"He made you human! No more ice queen."

"I am not an ice queen!"

"Not to me. But to guys, you sure are. Remember my brother?"

Suzanne felt all the blood drain out of her face.

"I didn't mean to hurt his feelings. I mean, he was nice and all, but he wanted me to talk about being a submissive wife."

"Oh, hey, I'm not judging. He's a little nutso. But," Kari added, perking up. "He's really doing well selling probiotics through multi-level marketing, and he and Junie are about to have their fourth child!"

In four years.

"Great! There's someone out there for everyone."

"I sure hope so." Kari eyed Mr. Tartan.

"And for some of us, there are someones."

"Mmm hmmm." Kari was in Scottish lumberjack land.

"Quit drooling," Suzanne ordered.

"It's my *job* to watch them!" Kari smirked.

"Mmm hmmm. So, I spent time with Andrew McCormick yesterday," she announced.

Carrot dangled.

"What?" Kari gave her full attention. "Was Amanda there?"

Carrot bitten.

"What is with you and your Amanda fascination? What the hell did she ever do to you to make you hate her so much?" Suzanne had never understood this. Then again, Suzanne didn't take business personally the way Kari did.

"She sniped a bunch of accounts from Fokused Shop-rite."

"Sniped?"

"You know."

"You mean her company presented their proposal and they won?"

"Yes."

"That's called competition, Kari. Not sniping."

Kari bared her teeth.

"You are unhinged about this woman."

"And now Consolidated Evalu-Shop got bought out by Anterdec. They're going to be a formidable force." Kari leaned in and whispered, "Are the floor mats at the entrance clean? I can't see from here and I have to answer that question on my app."

"Stand up and look!"

"If I do that I lose visual on Mr. Washboard Abs."

"Mr—ooooooh." Suzanne's voice trailed off to a hush as the employee who had been watering plants out front now changed lettering on a tall sign.

"I could rub my clothes all over that and get nice and wet."

"KARI!"

"Don't blow my cover!"

"I'm going to blow *chunks* if you keep talking like that." Suzanne gulped down half her now-warm Americano.

"What are you going to do with Gerald?"

Suzanne gave her the stink eye.

"I don't mean it that way. Get your mind out of the gutter."

"Get yours back on your job. You're not timing the intervals between customers," Suzanne pointed out. "Or measuring the curtains or whatever you're supposed to evaluate."

"I wish they'd ask me to see how easy it is to get an employee's phone number." Kari sighed. "You want a cinnamon bun? I have to buy one for the shop."

"I'll eat a few bites." Suzanne patted her stomach. "But not much."

Kari looked down at the swell of her hips, compared herself visually to Suzanne, and sighed.

"How do you live with so few carbs?"

"How do you live with so few morals?"

Kari cracked up, but her eyes tracked a guy walking past the big windows in the cafe. He wore a kilt, soccer cleats, and a tuxedo jacket.

No shirt.

"I love this neighborhood," she said with a sigh, looking away when the guy was gone.

"You love men."

"Guilty. So do you."

"Man. I lo—am attracted to one man. Not *men*."

"Just say you love Gerald, Suz. C'mon."

She said nothing.

"Are you seeing him tonight?"

"Yes." The giddy feeling that bubbled up every time she thought about another night, a breakfast, the domesticity of so many hours together in her home, made her feel lighter than air.

"And?"

"And what?"

Kari made an O with her index finger and thumb, and took her other finger and performed a vulgar gesture.

Suzanne smacked her hands down.

"You're sick."

"I'm sex-deprived."

Suzanne finished her coffee and stood, looking at Kari. "I have a client meeting and too many billable hours to log today. Thanks for the coffee."

177

"No 'thank you' for the advice?"

"What advice?"

Kari started to form that finger circle again.

Suzanne left, shaking her head.

The amusement ended abruptly four blocks away, when she got to the office and found a very pissed Norm Phelps at her desk, scowling.

"He called. He's donating."

"He who?"

"Gerald Wright."

"Already?"

"Called fifteen minutes ago. Asked for the firm's help in figuring out how to meet international and domestic law to forfeit the relic to a cultural institution."

Oh, my.

"Did you know about this?" Phelps' words came with a scorch mark.

"I suspected."

"You could have warned me."

"Why are you so invested, Norm? It's just an inheritance case."

"We have a buyer for the relic."

"We have two, technically. James McCormick has thrown his hat into the ring," she reminded him.

"The other buyer is determined," he snapped.

She shrugged. "And you think McCormick isn't? My client will make his own decisions. I can't sway him."

"You can make sure he's well informed."

"I've already done that." She frowned at him. "Are you implying otherwise?"

"No. But maybe you haven't spent enough time with him, going through the ins and outs, giving him a detailed sense of what the benefits of selling might entail."

"Why would I need to do that? It's cut and dried. Sell, make fifty to sixty million. Donate to a cultural institution. There isn't an in-between."

"He's just a chauffeur! His income is nothing. Why the hell would the guy choose any option but the wealthy one?" Norm ran a nervous hand through his hair.

"Not everyone is motivated by money."

"You sound like a second-year law student who's too earnest for her own good. Not a grizzled partner in a major Boston law firm, Suzanne."

"What bug crawled up your ass and died, Norm?"

"Harrison Kulli's client. The guy is well connected and he's making some shady threats."

"Like?"

"Let's just say it would behoove us all if Wright sold it to him."

"If I tell Gerald that, it's the fastest way to guarantee he *doesn't* sell to Kulli's client. You realize neither of us can stand Harrison Kulli."

"I don't give a shit whether you like the guy or not, Suz. I'm not asking you to be tennis partners. What I want is for this case to go away. And the easiest step is for Wright to sell the damn thing to Kulli's client."

"Or James McCormick."

Norm looked half dazed. "Shit."

"McCormick made an offer. Fifty million." She shrugged.

"Will he go higher?"

"I don't know."

Norm's eyes jumped from object to object in the room.

Her phone buzzed.

Ms. Dayton, this is Randita Murgheesi from the MFA. I can meet you at the Hopewell home to examine the item in question.

179

Surprised, she held up the phone to Norm. "An MFA staffer is offering to meet me regarding the relic."

Puzzled, he scowled. "Took them long enough. I thought they told you they'd never heard of it."

"Maybe they changed their minds? Worth a meeting."

What time? she typed back.

9pm was the reply. *Tonight.*

"That's late," she muttered.

"Probably a freelancer," Norm said with a sigh. "Can't hurt to get more information on it. Especially if Wright is just *donating* it," he added, sneering.

She texted Randita Murgheesi with a confirmation.

Suzanne then texted Gerald.

MFA called. Meeting at Hopewell place at 9pm with staffer. Kulli's gunning hard for his client, she typed, texting Gerald. *Can't get together tonight until much later.*

Come meet me after class. Playing pool with Declan and Vince, he texted back.

Who is Vince?

Buddy of mine. He's cool. You'll like him.

She grinned.

I'm coming, she wrote back. *If we're meeting the friends, this must be serious.*

It was serious the second you introduced me to Smoochy, he answered.

It was serious the first time I saw you, she thought.

And then she saw three dots.

...

We've been serious since the first time we met, Suz.

CHAPTER TWELVE

"Is that a love bite on your inner thigh, Declan?" Agnes' voice carried through the air like Joe Biden admiring a muscle car at a political rally in Lima, Ohio.

Declan looked down and rotated his hip just enough to scrutinize his own groin.

"Mercy mercy mercy," said a woman in the back row as she grabbed a small device and turned it on. A motorized whir filled the room.

"Jesus, Lindi, did you just turn on your vibrator?" Agnes called out.

"No! I would never bring that here," Lindi said, scandalized. "It's just my menopause fan."

"What's a menopause fan?" As the words escaped Declan McCormick's mouth, Gerald could see him wish he could pull them back in.

Too bad mouths didn't come with backspace keys.

"You're still young. Just wait. After Shannon pops out a few pups for you and her hormones go crazy in twenty years, you'll know damn well what a menopause fan is," Corrine said, then smiled sweetly.

"And lube!" Agnes crowed. "Everything heats up and then it dries out. Maybe all the hormones evaporate all that—" she waved her hands vaguely over her midsection, "—stuff."

Declan's face was frozen in a mask of horror, like Chris Christie at a Trump rally.

The door to the classroom opened. Gerald searched the room, taking a fast headcount. No one else should be here. But hey—he'd welcome any intrusion right about now.

"Hellllooooooooo!" called out a familiar voice.

Marie Jacoby.

Years ago, Gerald had worked security at a store along the Macy's Thanksgiving Day Parade path. A float had snagged on a telephone pole and folded in half.

Declan McCormick did a damn fine naked imitation of that float just now.

And then he paused, mid-fold, and opened up, like a flower.

Marie shrieked.

"You really *are* naked! Agnes told me you were a nude model in this class and I didn't believe her!"

"Why *wouldn't* you believe me?" Agnes burst out.

"Says the woman who sold me a dime bag of oregano passed off as marijuana!" Marie shouted.

Tortured gasps filled the classroom, followed by hushed whispers.

Corrine frowned. "Hey. Wait a minute." She glared at Agnes. "That bud you sold me wasn't really bud?"

If Gerald didn't do something, the class was about to descend into uncontrollable chaos.

"Now Marie, I told you my grandson's in trouble for that," Agnes said in a contrite voice.

"For the weed being oregano, or for selling pot at all?"

"Both. But mostly for it being oregano. He said he had no idea."

"Marie," Gerald said gruffly, moving between her and the rest of the class to act as a barrier. "How can I help you? You're interrupting my class."

"'Marie,' is it? So I've gone from 'Mrs. Jacoby' to 'Marie.' That's awfully familiar of you, Gerald, considering I'm your boss's mother-in-law." The woman clearly needed to preserve some dignity. Behind him,

182

Gerald heard the distinct shuffling sound of Declan putting on a robe.

The groans of protest from the class were a hint, too.

"No, ma'am. Declan's not my boss any longer. And we're not in James McCormick's home right now." He paused for emphasis, planting his hands on his hips in a gesture of dominance. "You're on my turf."

"Oh." She frowned. "That's right." She gave him a bright smile. "Marie it is!" Her eyes crawled over him appreciatively, with a cold inventory that would make a less hardened man squirm. "Do you do yoga? Want some free passes to my class?"

Was she checking out his butt?

"I train at a gym, Marie. My workouts are all very basic. It's all about lifting."

She blinked, eyes on his arms. "I'll bet it is, but yoga can help with core strength and stretching. Balance is paramount for good lift technique, you know."

"I do."

"At your gym, are there more men...like you?"

"More chauffeurs?"

She tittered. "More, you know—big guys who could use a little downward dog."

Every sentence out of this woman's mouth sounded porny.

"I can ask around."

"You do that."

"Why are you here, Marie?"

"Agnes has been avoiding my class ever since she sold me that oregano. It's time for a throw down."

He looked at Agnes.

Looked at Marie.

"The woman is ninety and looks like an artifact from the MFA's Mayan Civilization exhibit, Marie. You're going to fight her?"

183

"She cheated me! And she's ninety-two. She really has no excuse. You live that long, you're supposed to be filled with wisdom. Not bullshit."

"It was an honest mistake!" Agnes shouted, moving behind Corrine.

"No, no you don't," Corrine protested. "You don't get to use me as a human shield again, Agnes. I lost some of my weave the last time."

The *last* time?

"Look, this is a community-based art class and you're interrupting, Marie."

"But my son-in-law is in here! And Agnes needs to be taught a lesson."

"The only lessons being taught in here are by me." Gerald had learned years ago how to use his body as a weapon without touching the target. Guiding her through nonverbal cues, he made Marie Jacoby take one step backwards.

One was all he needed. Once you open that door, you can shoo an annoying fly out.

"But I—"

"Enrollment is closed. We don't have any space in the class." Blocking unruly people was an art, too.

She took another step back.

"I don't want to be a student! Even I draw the line at ogling my naked son-in-law!"

"Glad to know you *have* a line, Marie," Declan called out.

"Can't I just stay and finish my business with Agnes?"

"You're welcome to a chair in the hall."

She moved slowly, but Gerald wasn't worried. Inertia set in when you glared at someone, puffed out your shoulders, planted your hands on your hips, and most important—

Didn't back down.

184

"This isn't fair!" she finally squeaked as Gerald reached for the door, her body halfway in, halfway out of the room."

"My classroom. My rules."

"Then you're a dictator!" she said in outrage.

"The Clay Dictator." He grinned. "I like the sound of that." Her face flashed through the small mesh-glass window, screwed up in furious confusion.

Click.

Declan McCormick did a slow clap.

So did Agnes.

"You!" Gerald said, jabbing a finger in Agnes' direction. "Deal with her after class."

"You can't get away with this, Agnes!" Marie's muffled voice came through the door. "I will hunt you down and I will find you and I will..." Her voice trailed off.

"Over oregano?" Declan shook his head slowly. "She sounds like Liam Neeson in the movie *Taken* over *oregano?*"

Gerald and Declan shared a shrug.

Declan dropped the robe.

As Gerald walked from student to student, admiring technique, correcting proportions, using his voice and hands to guide, he studied his former boss—and now, friend. Inviting him to be a model had been natural. A few years ago, he'd been asked what he did in his free time, and when he'd mentioned sculpting, the conversation had ventured into issues of finding people comfortable enough to pose.

Declan McCormick, of all people, had offered.

Gerald had accepted.

And here they were, on their fifth course together.

The guy's body was fabulous as a subject, but to Gerald, all bodies were fabulous. Short, tall, lean, plump, old, young—the endless fascination with all the variations and permutations of the human form didn't stop just because a body didn't meet society's standards of beauty.

He rejected those standards. They were false, based on commercial and corporate ideals.

His next model was a seventy-eight-year-old great-grandmother who had scars down one thigh from being dragged for a quarter mile during civil rights protests in the 1960s.

Beauty came in all forms.

His criteria for modeling in his class were simple: Twenty-five bucks an hour, ninety minutes of holding still, no silly giggling over being nude.

Declan waived the fee.

By the end of class, Gerald was uncharacteristically wiped. Normally, teaching refueled him.

Reconnecting with Suzanne, plus the burden of the inheritance, led to an emotional gravity he struggled to manage.

Earlier that day, he'd made his decision: donate the relic. Have Suzanne's firm figure out the international law intricacies. He wanted it to go to the right cultural institution so it could be preserved, studied, honored and used to understand old civilizations.

But the weight of that decision hadn't lifted the burden.

A night of shooting pool with Vince and Declan should be just the ticket. He looked forward to watching Dec and Vince spar.

As students filed out of the room, he felt a strong hand clutch his arm. Turning around, he found dead air.

He had to look way down.

"Gerald, I want to tell you how much I enjoy this class." Agnes' voice trembled slightly, though it always did. This time, the tone made him pause, his soles pressing into the ground, his body relaxing into being more present.

"Thank you."

"You make it fun. An old woman like me needs more fun in her life." Were her eyes filling with actual tears?

"Of course you do," he said with compassion.

"So please, please don't have Louise Johnson as your nude model for the next class. She may be young and have a tighter body than mine, but she's no Declan McCormick."

Sigh. "How do you know her name?" He was about to mention that Louise wasn't young, but to a ninety-two-year-old woman, a seventy-eight year old must seem "young."

"We're both docents at the same museum. She farts a lot."

"Agnes," he said in a low warning voice.

"I'm just saying. We'll need to wear charcoal face masks if you have that woman in here," she continued. "Her doctor told her to cut out dairy, but nooooooo. Louise knows better!"

"I'm not having this conversation."

"She's so selfish," Agnes grumbled. "Always thinking about herself."

He saw Corrine pause at the doorway and look back.

"Are you lying about Louise again?" Corrine called out. "You're just jealous Gerald didn't ask you."

"I'm not taking off my clothes to let a bunch of people have fantasies about my body."

"Fantasies!" Corrine hooted. "More like nightmares. When people our age are naked, we look like human being candles all melted down."

"It's all beautiful, ladies," he assured them.

They eyed him like predators. "When it's tight and young and works well and balances out, it sure is, Gerald. But wait. Just wait."

"I'm enjoying the journey just like you. One day at a time."

"I'll be a nude model!" Corrine piped up. "What's it pay?"

"Twenty-five an hour. Plus you get a free class here at the arts center."

"That's it? *Playboy* models make tens of thousands!" Agnes grumbled.

"I'm not Hugh Hefner," Gerald joked.

Fifty million dollars, a voice inside him whispered.

Huh. Maybe he was closer than he thought.

"Quit stalling. Marie's still out here, just waiting for you." Corrine caught Gerald's eye. "I love a good catfight."

"You're my second, Corrine," Agnes said as she caught up to her, grumbling. "If I need you to fight in my place, go for her eyes. She wears contacts. One good jab and..."

Gerald shut the door.

With relief.

Bzzz.

A text from Suzanne.

"Hey!" Declan called out from the dressing room. "We're still shooting pool with your friend?"

"Yeah."

"Cool." Declan strode out into the classroom. Tonight, he'd shown up in casual clothes from the start.

Gerald looked at his phone.

Be there around ten. Maybe sooner. See you soon.

He grinned.

"I take it Suzanne's coming, too?" Declan asked.

"How'd you guess?"

"The stupid lovesick grin on your face."

"That's how you looked the day you came out of that bagel shop when you met Shannon." Gerald almost said *sir* again.

"Did I?" Declan assumed his stone face. "I thought I looked like this."

"Not that day."

They shared a smile.

Ten minutes later, they waited for a free pool table, drinking beers and riling each other up about who would beat whom.

Vince appeared.

Vince didn't just walk into bars. Vince parted the Red Sea when he entered any establishment. Enormous, covered in tattoos and scars, and with the air of a convict who lords over all the prisoners and guards in a maximum security joint, Vince was in*vinc*ible.

His parents got his name right.

"Hey," Vince shouted. "G!"

Declan's eyes flew wide open and he looked up.

Way up.

"Hold on. This is Vince? My brother's personal trainer *Vince*?"

Vince reached for Declan's hand and shook him like a rag doll. "Another McCormick bitch! Good to meet you, man. Boy, I see who has all the muscle in your family." He eyed Declan and let out a low whistle.

Declan looked pleased.

"Not you," Vince clarified. "Andrew's a wuss, but *he* is bulking up."

"First half of that is right," Declan shot back. He puffed up like a peacock-cobra hybrid.

Vince held out his palms. "No offense, man. Just calling it like I see it."

Considering Vince's arms were the size of most men's thighs, he really did walk the walk.

189

Eyes narrowing, Declan took Vince in. "You a pool shark like your buddy?"

He held up hands like bear paws. "Do these look like precision tools?"

Declan grinned. "Hope you brought enough to cover the drinks, because you're losing."

Gerald cleared his throat with meaning.

"I'm onto you," Declan said. "You play innocent."

Gerald racked the balls and they started.

Someone's phone buzzed. As all three checked, Declan held up one finger, turned on his heel, and walked out the main door. Business.

"Heard he left Anterdec. Bought some coffee chain. Thinks he's going to build the next Starbucks," Vince said as Gerald took his shot, spreading the balls but not getting any where he wanted them.

"Yeah. Works his ass off."

"Don't we all?"

Gerald's phone buzzed.

You two play this round. Need to manage an issue for fifteen minutes.

The text was from Declan.

"He's out for this game. Says he'll be back in fifteen."

Vince snorted and took his shot. "Their lives really suck." The scratch ball went in the right corner pocket.

"So does your aim."

Fishing the ball out of the pocket with hands better suited for picking up small cars, Vince grumbled a string of unintelligible syllables.

"Billionaires with plenty of money but no time to enjoy it. Being rich means being busy," Vince finally said.

Gerald stayed silent.

"Hey, man—take your shot. Waiting for an engraved invitation?"

Gerald took his shot. The ball rolled aimlessly to the edge and stopped, an inch from target.

"So close, yet so far. How're things with Suzanne? You tell her the truth yet?"

Shit. Vince didn't just go straight to the heart of the matter. He went to the bone.

"What?"

"Your biggest fear. You told me the other day. Remember?"

Silence.

"You have to tell her."

"I did."

"The whole story?" Vince raised an eyebrow as he elegantly shot the striped nine into the right side pocket.

"Most of it."

"'Most' is not 'whole.' You graduated college. You should know that."

"Not talking about this, Vince."

"That's your problem, Gerald. It's how you lost her ten years ago. By not talking about it."

"I'm not one of your clients."

"I'm telling you this as a *friend*."

They stared at each other.

Bzzz.

Text from Suzanne.

Kulli is here. Hopewell house. Weird. Might be late.

And that was it.

"Shit." Fire poured through his veins.

Vince picked up on it immediately.

"I have to go," he said curtly.

"Afraid you'll lose to...." Vince's voice dropped off. "What's wrong?"

"Nothing. Something. I have to go meet Suzanne."

He sprinted, hearing Vince call out, "Be whole!"

Kulli wouldn't be stupid enough to hurt Suzanne.

He knew that.

What Gerald feared was worse.

Kulli might tell her the *whole* truth about why he left her.

And once again, Gerald hadn't trusted her with the truth.

No. That wasn't right.

Gerald didn't have the guts to tell her the truth.

CHAPTER THIRTEEN

The Hopewell mansion *wasn't*. Suzanne had to laugh as she pulled into a rare parking spot on the Back Bay and realized she was about to go to your basic townhouse in a long row of them. Hopewell had more money than James McCormick but lived a life under the radar.

She admired that.

The artifact rested in a small case, under glass, in a room one walked into, surrounded by subdued security that Suzanne knew was high tech and designed to be inconspicuous. The relic wasn't the only item on display, but she forced herself not to pay attention to the others.

They weren't her focus.

Footsteps. The carpet muted them, but she heard the steady beats as they slowed. The person was clearly coming closer. Security? The person from the MFA? Prepared to turn around, she halted as the person spoke.

"Hello, Suzanne. Fancy meeting you here."

Her shoulders hunched. She fought to lower them. When a guy like Harrison Kulli approaches you from behind, any movement, any show of emotion was a sign of weakness. Guys like him thrived on it.

On reaction.

On knowing they'd gotten to you, even in the smallest of ways.

"Harrison," she said. Trying to play it cool, she reached for her phone, quickly typing a few words to Gerald. She hit Send and slowly put the phone back in her purse.

"Recognized me by my voice, did you?"

"No. By the faint scent of brimstone."

He laughed through his nose, but the sound was tight. She'd gotten to him.

Good.

"I'm hardly the devil."

"No. You're not intelligent enough. But you'll do as one of his minions."

And with that, she spun around on her heel, taking great care to look down in order to make eye contact.

He was pissed. You had to have spent two years under his command to know that, though. A stranger would see a placid man, a face that gave no quarter.

Harrison Kulli was a compact man, wiry and strong, Standing at about five foot three inches, he exuded anger. It radiated out of him like musk.

That quality had been fabulous in battle, commanding troops.

In civilian life it had only one truly good purpose.

A purpose used by men in power.

Suzanne had done her research, trying to figure out who Kulli worked for. She'd failed. Whoever his client was, the cloak of anonymity was secure.

She didn't much care. She knew what Gerald would decide. But Kulli's presence definitely complicated the matter. Over the years, she'd come to wonder whether he'd played a role in Gerald's leaving her. Call it a hunch. Or intuition.

Maybe just a grudge.

Because Kulli had hit on her more than once out in the desert.

Luckily, the guy took *no*—twice—for an answer.

Barely.

"Gerald isn't with you?"

"I can't speak about my client. Confidentiality."

"Listen to you. Such a lawyer. I never pegged you for a shark."

She studied him, not giving in. The less said, the better.

"You look the same, Harrison." That was designed to be a blow. The guy had clearly bulked up, arms bursting out of an expensive Armani suit. He looked nothing like the rat he'd been years ago.

"The last decade's been good to me," he countered, making sure to flash his Rolex.

Were watches the new in-person dick pic?

Steve Raleigh. That's who he reminded her of.

Harrison Kulli was a slimier version of Steve Raleigh.

Nothing about Kulli's demeanor made her afraid. They were in the exhibition room with two armed guards at the entrance, dressed in plain clothes. Given the amount of objects of high value, and the rotation of estate lawyers and appraisers, heirs and household staff, she knew Kulli wouldn't do anything to put her in harm's way.

His very presence, though, and that question about Gerald gave her pause.

"If you'll excuse me, I'm here to meet with a representative from the Museum of Fine Arts," she declared, making it clear this conversation was over.

"You're looking at him."

"You're Randita Mugheeri?" Her glare held nothing back.

"Actually, I am. Your phone number was easy to find, if you know where to look."

Adrenaline shot through her. She conspicuously looked at the guards. Both were the same men she'd recognized from the other day. She pulled out her phone and dialed 9-1-1 without pressing Send.

Always be prepared.

"You two back together again?" he asked, the casual tone jarring.

"What?"

"You and Gerald. You two back together?"

"Mr. Wright is my client," she said frostily, starting to walk toward the door to leave. This was a set-up.

"'Mr. Wright'? Aren't you getting fancy, Suzanne. Most people don't refer to their ex-fiancé like that. Then again, after what he did to you..."

All those years ago, she'd been tight-lipped. Had not said a word to anyone about how Gerald had broken up with her. Only Kari and her parents had known.

A cold flush covered her body, heart hot inside her chest.

She didn't respond. Bait. He was baiting her.

"I can understand it, though."

She held her breath.

"You do know why he broke it off with you, right?" His voice was like poison ivy coated in velvet.

"Mr. Wright is my client in the capacity of—"

"He never told you, did he?" Kulli inhaled slowly, the sound passing over his back teeth like a snake's hiss.

Say nothing, she screamed inside. *He's playing a dangerous psych game.*

"He stole the relic. Stole it, and brought it home when his mother was sick. Came back and was with you for just a few more months before he was discharged. Gerald was never the same. You know I counseled him?"

Suzanne fought back the snort of disbelief that rose up in her.

"He held on. The curse got to him, though."

"Curse?" She infused as much condescension as possible into one word.

"Yeah, curse. That damned relic may be one of the oldest objects with writing on it ever found, Suz."

Don't call me Suz, she thought.

"He was never the same after he brought it back. And then the nightmares about you started."

"What are you talking ab—" Damn it. He'd succeeded.

He knew it, too.

"Got your attention, didn't it? Convince him to sell to my client and I'll tell you everything you need to know."

"I can't ethically do that and you know it."

"You can't ethically handle a nearly-priceless relic that doesn't exist, Suz. Don't take the moral high ground here."

"We're done, Kulli. I won't advise my client to take action he doesn't want to take."

"He'd be stupid to give it all up. Just like when he gave you up. That's what Wright does, though. He cuts and runs. Once he donates that relic, he'll disappear again."

Her throat seized.

Kulli knew he'd hit a nerve. "Didn't think about that, did you? If he has a big pot of money following him around, he can't run off. But if he donates, he leaves. Just like he left you ten years ago."

"Shut up."

"Not so much power now, huh, Suzanne? You always were easy to break. Wright, too. It's not too late, though. My client wants that relic. Wants it bad. He'll go to $60 million."

"I'll advise Mr. Wright."

"Why are you so loyal to him?"

"He is my client," she persisted.

"After what he wanted to do to you?"

Years of law school and legal work had attuned her to the subtleties of language.

"*Wanted* to do to me?"

197

Kulli's eyes went hooded, mouth curling in contempt. "I was his CO. He spilled his guts one night. I know why he needed to leave. And why he broke it off with you."

"I know that, too. PTSD. It happens to the best of men and women who serve in combat."

"Worst, too," Kulli said sourly.

"You don't need to illuminate me, Harrison. Whatever you think you're accomplishing with this conversation, you're not—"

Commotion in the outer hall made her turn sharply, head ringing with Kulli's words and the not-so-distant sound of men arguing.

And then Gerald rushed into the room, eyes wild, body primed to fight.

Wearing a gun.

"Gerald couldn't stop thinking about *killing* you, Suzanne," Kulli said, his voice soft and compassionate, but his eyes alight with an evil joy at delivering the shocking emotional blow to her. He completely ignored Gerald, but she realized with dawning disgust that Gerald was his real audience. "That's why he left. He was being driven crazy by thoughts of killing *you*."

Very carefully, Gerald moved his hands from his chest holster, and then moved like a flash of lightning as security guards poured into the room.

Seconds too late.

The blow rolled out in slow motion, Kulli's clean-shaven jaw hooking left so fast it seemed like it was a separate body part from the rest of him, as if it would have ricocheted off a far wall if the layer of skin stretched over bone hadn't been there. Gerald's mouth stretched, more teeth showing than she thought a face should have as he grimaced in battle, a glint of gold from a back molar shining in the room's overhead light.

A spray of Kulli's blood, a long drop gone to spatter, hit her directly on the exposed skin above the V of her shirt, a drop sliding down between her breasts.

Mayhem.

Mayhem *erupted*.

Kulli centered himself quickly, bending his knees, arms whipped into fight mode, his suit jacket pulled tight around the elbows and shoulders, an impediment as seconds turned into minutes. Without any such obstacle, Gerald's blows were rapid fire, like a machine gun array, rat-a-tat-tat, *punch punch punch*.

"STOP IT!" she screamed, her reaction to Kulli's revelation truncated by the rush of fight hormones that coursed through her as she started to reach for Gerald, to pull him off, as his fist smashed into Kulli's eye once, twice, and then they were down on the ground, a mass of enraged muscle and senseless breaths, grunts and groans and blows filling the air.

Guards poured into the room, six of them on top of Gerald and Kulli, the mass of body parts and movement and blood a bastardized version of the old kids' game, Twister.

Only these guards had guns, zip-tie handcuffs, and authority.

Within seconds Gerald was on the ground, gun removed, face down, wrists cuffed, with Kulli screaming, "He started it! Check the video!"

And then Kulli kicked Gerald in the head, the thump of shoe against skull making a sickening sound like a melon dropped from a rooftop. Gerald twitched, then slumped against the carpet, out cold.

Red rage filled her vision.

Two guards dragged Kulli away from Gerald as she advanced, throwing off her jacket, ready to do damage.

She stopped.

She breathed.

She closed her eyes, the cacophony too much.

Enough damage had been done. Jail for her wouldn't help Gerald, and could be career suicide. Barely able to manage her impulse control, she struggled, but found the place inside that said to stop.

The place Gerald couldn't access ten seconds ago.

She couldn't blame him. If what Kulli said was true...

Dropping to the floor, she checked Gerald. Pulse was fine. Breathing was regular. He had blood from cuts on his knuckles, but was otherwise okay.

Being a former medic had its pluses.

"I'm pressing charges!" Kulli screamed.

"You just kicked him unconscious!" she roared, searching her jacket for her cell phone, pressing Send to complete the 9-1-1 call she'd primed earlier.

"He started it!"

"And you finished it while his arms were tied behind his back? You fucking sick piece of cowardly shit," she said, her voice dangerously low.

In the end, it didn't matter.

The police hauled Gerald off to jail.

But damned if she didn't get them to take Kulli, too.

Video works both ways.

* * *

Bailing her ex-fiancé out of jail after he assaulted their former commanding officer in front of a rare artifact that could change the world's understanding of its origins wasn't on her Google calendar for the day, but Suzanne did it anyhow.

"Thank you," he muttered as she pulled him aside roughly and examined his injuries under a blinking fluorescent light.

"Ow!" Her fingers pressed against the butterfly bandage. Kulli's kick had split his eyebrow. A red spot where the toe had connected with the temple wasn't pretty and would go through the bruise color cycle over the next two weeks.

"If you think that hurts, just wait."

"What does that mean?" he grumbled.

She walked away. Marched out into the cold urban landscape where she'd rather talk to a homeless guy than Gerald right now.

He followed her.

Slowly, but he did.

"What in the hell did you think you were doing back there, Gerald?" She whipped around, heedless of passersby.

"Rescuing you!"

"I don't need to be rescued, damn it! I need to be loved. Trusted. Was Kulli telling the truth?"

He flinched, eyes stormy, changing color second by second as he reacted to her words.

"Yes." He sighed. "I can explain."

"You should have done that ten years ago."

"I *couldn't*."

"You couldn't trust me with the truth," she said softly, her voice dropping, all her energy pouring out of her. "Nothing you could have *told* me would have been worse than what you *did* to me. Shutting me out was more painful than killing me, Gerald. It was its own death, only worse, because I had to live with the pain."

He closed his eyes, cutting her off from the view of his emotions. "I know that now."

"But you didn't reach out. Didn't try to reconnect."

"I assumed you hated me after I ended things like that."

"I did. For a long, long time. I knew something was wrong. You don't come out of that hellhole without being screwed up in so many ways," she said, choking back a sick laugh. "And I guessed it had to do with PTSD. Intrusive thoughts. Dreams. Nightmares."

"Never intrusive thoughts," he insisted, his voice hoarse with emotion. "I never had actual...images...or fantasies of...."

He seemed to need her to know that. She nodded.

"Just because you dream something doesn't mean you want it to happen."

"Jesus, Suzanne, it was the opposite. I couldn't get the fucking dreams out of my sleep. So I stopped sleeping."

"Which really helped," she said with a wry smile. "I'm sure."

"I went mad. Crazy. And the fleeting sleep I did have was filled with dreams of hurting you." He looked at her with such rawness, such tender pain, that Suzanne felt the wind knocked out of her. Once in a while, during litigation, Suzanne had moments where every thought in her head drained out of her at once, abandoning her to a world of eyes and judgment. She would stand still, horrified by her muteness, completely incapable of putting together a coherent sentence.

Over the years she'd learned to weather those moments, and to trust that her brain's hiccup would end.

She had no idea her heart could hiccup, too.

"You hurt me emotionally in unfathomable ways to prevent yourself from hurting me with your hands?"

"You could put it that way."

"I just did."

"Then yes."

"I wish you'd told me. I wouldn't have left."

"I knew that. Which is exactly why I did leave. If I'd stayed, I would have dragged you through everything. Every crazy bit of it."

"I had my own crazy, too."

"Not like me, Suz. Not like me."

202

Haunted men have a similar look. Their eyes go hollow and ragged. Women, too, except the look is more subtle. Muted. Trained from childhood to smile, to please, grown women who go through trauma have a pained friendliness that belies what's underneath.

Men aren't held to the same standards.

But Suzanne could still see the trauma in him.

"Has ten years been long enough?"

"For what?"

"To heal?"

"Yes. I have better tools in my coping toolbox. I know how to handle life. I didn't at first."

The isolation, the loneliness, the outright madness he must have felt all those years ago, driven to leave her in order to protect her, made her ache.

And pissed.

But mostly sad. So sad.

Another sliver of anger peeled off her, floating on the wind, carried far away like wood shavings in the hands of a fine woodcarver.

This was a breaking point. Years ago, he'd broken her. She'd put herself back together and gone on, but even now she had to admit to herself how much she hadn't gotten over him. How the hole had remained, though she'd learned to live with it. His revelation meant nothing.

Truly.

"Do you know how hard it was to leave you? In my own twisted logic, I was sure I made the right decision. But people who aren't thinking right are, by definition, unable to make good decisions." His look was feral. "I was a lost cause. I was damned either way, so I thought that picking the one way that wouldn't damn you, too, was the best choice."

"And I hated you for it. All these years, I've hated you for it."

"I understand."

"And loved you, too. Not for making that decision. Just for being you. Just—"

"I know," he said softly, respecting the space between them, not closing. She loved him for that, too. "I know."

"Look at me," she demanded, forcing his eyes to stay on hers. "You just told me your biggest secret. Your biggest fear. And I'm still here. Right here."

His throat shook as he swallowed.

"See? Whatever you thought would happen, didn't."

He nodded, closing his eyes, the wave of emotion that coursed across his skin a kinesthetic sign of the emotional tsunami underneath.

"You never looked me up?" she asked.

"I knew you went to Michigan for law school. Then I stopped looking."

"You had no idea I've been in Boston for more than seven years?"

He shook his head, then winced, holding his palm against his jaw. "No."

"We've been in the same city for seven years and never crossed paths."

"We did indirectly. Who do you think drove Declan and Andrew to those family trust meetings?"

The space between them closed as she took a step toward him. "I had no idea."

One step. He took one step, too.

The space was halved.

"I would never hurt you, Suzanne. Never. I'd die before I'd let anyone hurt you, including me."

"I know."

"And I'm sorry."

"I know."

Could she do this? The funny part was that the dreams he had—hurting her?—didn't matter. Not one iota. It was the secrecy. The shame he felt in telling her. Was that still there?

"Were you going to tell me? Before Kulli beat you to it?"

"Yes."

She believed him, and not just because she wanted to believe him.

A soft laugh, sardonic and bittersweet, escaped her. "You're in so much legal trouble for assaulting Kulli."

Gerald gave a half smile. "I know a great lawyer."

She groaned, the moment changing, the feeling in the air between them shifting to that sense that they lived in their own bubble, a place where the rest of the world whooshed on around them. Where balance came naturally and they were understood.

"I don't take criminal cases."

"I'm a criminal? Huh." He stared at her. "Ever date a bad boy?"

"No. I only date good guys. Men in uniform."

"There's a first time for everything."

The kiss was tender, his lips bruised. She tasted copper, a hint of blood, and his mouth tightened.

"You have to admit, hitting him was cathartic," she said, squeezing his hips.

His hand brushed her hair over her shoulder, the knuckles raw. "I was stupid."

"We'll get the charges dropped."

"I love you." Even when they'd been together, he'd said it rarely. To hear it now was unbelievable, like breaking the sound barrier with your heart.

"I love you too, Gerald." He leaned in for another kiss, but instead she punched his chest.

"What's that for?"

"For not trusting me. For wasting ten years."

"How many punches do you want? I deserve it." Braced for impact, he closed his eyes, then opened one.

Groaning, she reached for his hand and began walking. "Let's go."

"Where?"

"Home."

CHAPTER FOURTEEN

"You strike me as the kind of man who wants to earn his success. Not have it handed to him. I admire that." A week later, Gerald was working, driving James McCormick to a meeting at a venture capital firm on the 128 belt outside of Boston.

He'd just rejected James McCormick's offer of seventy million for the relic.

"I'll donate to the cultural institution of your choice —law permitting—on one condition," Gerald offered, wondering if the old man would bite.

If James McCormick admired him, might as well go for the gold.

Er, so to speak.

"What's that?"

"The Montgomery Foundation agrees to sponsor the Westside Center for the Arts in perpetuity. All programs, plus a to-be-determined number of camp scholarships." He quoted their annual budget.

"I spend that on fine dining in a year, Gerald," McCormick scoffed. "And you're asking my sons to use Elena's family money to support your center."

James McCormick's eyes met Gerald's in the rearview mirror, one of his bushy white eyebrows cocked. He looked just like his son, Andrew, in that moment.

"Why should I care what you do with that artifact? And why would I stake charity money on your decision?

If you wanted that kind of investment, you could have asked for it without the contingency."

Gerald had just swallowed his pride to ask.

Now he swallowed a lump in his throat.

"Then it's a done deal?"

James harumphed. "Talk to Becky tomorrow. She'll arrange the details."

"Thank you."

"No need to thank me. You know I grew up in South Boston." He didn't add qualifiers to any of his comments or questions. Gerald admired that.

"Yes, sir."

"I wish we'd had a club for arts and recreation. Instead, we used cans and sticks." He gave a strange grin. "My children had fencing coaches and ski lessons."

"We work to give our kids a life that's better than the one we had, sir."

"That we do. That we most certainly do. Do you have children, Gerald?"

He thought of Suzanne.

"Not yet."

"We never planned for three." James McCormick's voice was unusually wistful. "Elena and I were surprised by her pregnancy with Terry. It's not that he wasn't wanted. Just, well...unexpected. A bit early, you might say. We didn't have the time together that most husbands and wives cherish before focusing on building businesses and families."

Gerald said nothing.

"And then Declan two years later, and Andrew after that. Blessed with three healthy boys, we used to say. Elena wished we'd had a girl—said I would have spoiled her rotten. That men like me needed a 'daddy's little girl.'"

Gerald watched covertly in the rearview mirror. McCormick's stare was unfocused, his mind wrapped up in memory. "But no such luck. Three boys it was for us."

"They are all fine men, if I may say so, sir," Gerald said, meaning it.

"Thank you. I agree. It does a man good to know he's built something with a strong foundation. From the ground up. And while the result is never perfect, neither is the journey, Gerald. All we can do is our best."

Our best.

"You decided what to do with that relic long ago, Gerald. That's evident. Eleven years ago you made sure it made it to safety. I never thought you'd actually sell it to me."

"What—you—you knew? You knew that I was the one who..."

"Who smuggled the relic into the U.S. from Afghanistan? Yes."

"How?"

"Background check."

"Background check? No background check would reveal that part of my life," he argued.

"The kind Anterdec does most certainly would. And did. You weren't hired to be a chauffeur, Gerald. You're part of our crack security team. And when I found out what you did, and how Hopewell ended up with the relic, I decided to hire you on the spot."

"I always wondered why Anterdec hired me."

"In spite of your shaky past, you mean?"

McCormick hit the bullseye.

"Yes."

"I'll admit, hiring an ex-Navy SEAL who'd spent nearly two months on an inpatient psych ward was not my vision of the ideal candidate as security detail for my company," McCormick said. Understatement of the year. McCormick was a judgmental bastard. Gerald knew it.

So did the old man.

"And if that were all we dug up, you never would have made it to the first interview. Fortunately, our team knows that I have a nuanced view on people."

Gerald struggled not to snort, smirk, snicker or guffaw.

"And when I learned you violated federal and international law for the sake of a higher good, I knew you needed to be on Anterdec's team."

"Good to know." He frowned. "If you already knew I was the one with the relic, why did you call Suzanne and ask?"

The old man's eyes clouded with confusion. "That's funny. I asked Suzanne to come to my house because Declan recommended it."

"Declan?"

"He never mentioned you were the heir."

"I never told him."

"Then why would he suggest I call Suzanne and..."

Their eyes met in the rearview mirror.

James McCormick chuckled. "Declan as matchmaker. I never would have thought it."

Good thing Declan wasn't Gerald's boss anymore.

Because he was a dead man.

* * *

"You have to give Declan McCormick credit. It worked, right? He got me to show up and run into you at his father's house." It was morning, and she was at his place, her friend Kari promising to walk Suzanne's dog while she spent the night here. His place wasn't much compared to hers, but it was home.

His home.

Soon they'd have *their* home.

But no one was in a rush.

"James was in on it, too, in his own way. He'd known about the relic all those years." Naked and sleepy, they took their time under the covers, talking and playing, the casual way she let the sheet slip off her breasts a simple pleasure. He hadn't been this intimate with her *ever*. They were in new territory now, and so far, both had taken to it with such natural grace that it seemed too good to be true.

Gerald loved the access he had to her body. Couldn't wait to make her his muse.

Again.

The long, pale torso had always fascinated him, her ribs stretching out in a line of gridded perfection, as if she'd been given more bones than usual. Strong, lean legs that felt perfect around his waist at just the right moments. Arms with the right tone and slim surgeon's hands. Her hair was honey and her eyes were ocean. She'd always hated her freckles but for him they were a map, points on a canvas, a speckled layering of character.

When she smiled, she lit the world.

"It's all good," Gerald said with a sigh. "I got McCormick to fund the arts center forever."

"And paperwork shows McCormick had been trying to buy it from Hopewell for ages. Maybe he saw an opportunity."

"We already had a meeting set up for that day! And Declan hates when other people meddle in his and Shannon's lives. I've heard him grumble about it in the back of the limo for years. His wife and mother-in-law are Olympic champions in Meddling."

"They medaled in meddling?" she joked.

He groaned at the terrible wordplay.

"Meddling got us here." Her hand moved from his knee between his legs, the slow quality of her journey reassuring, sensual in its timing. She knew how to hold him, stroke him, make him feel a rising urgency that was tempered now.

Calibrated by the knowledge that this wasn't going away.

And that she wasn't a dream that would soon end in nightmares.

Since they'd reunited, the dreams had faded again, consigned to a back corner of his subconscious.

"It all worked out for the best. The Afghani officials are over the moon about the relic. You donated it, and now your hands are washed of it. No charges against you, and Kulli's being investigated for antiquities fraud."

"Plus there's the clause in the will," Gerald reminded her.

"I couldn't tell you." In the event that Gerald did donate the relic, Harold Hopewell had set aside a $100,000 inheritance for him. Suzanne wasn't allowed to mention the clause—per Hopewell's instructions—until or unless Gerald decided to donate.

"I know. A happy surprise."

"You're keeping it, right?"

"Some of it, sure. Enough to get out of debt and donate a little to the center." It wasn't enough for Gerald to retire on, but it would accelerate the timeline for him to be able to just be an artist all day.

"Nice," she said.

"But the McCormicks already funded the center and some camps, so..."

"What's it like to work for the McCormicks?" she asked, making Gerald vibrate with amusement. Completely nude, their limbs twisted against each other, her smooth thigh found his, the delight of hair against bare skin a sensory buffet. He couldn't stop touching her, hands caressing, eyes absorbing. He was readying for an art project.

Later, he thought.

Later she would pose.

"You know what it's like. You work for them, too."

Her own eyes took him in, hungry for more. What did he look like to her? He'd bulked up these ten years, his shoulders bulging with strength, legs built like cabled powerhouses, thick and sturdy. Veins bulged over well-defined, taut skin. He was smiling, his cheeks red, his morning stubble coming in a cinnamon red that had always surprised her.

She sat up on one elbow, head propped in one palm, her face a delight. "I sit across from Declan, Andrew and Terry McCormick once a year. It's hardly the same as what you do. You probably run period errands for their wives and girlfriends."

The bed convulsed as he shifted, staring at her in shock.

"How did you know?"

She just laughed. "I assumed. Plus, you have no shame. Remember that time at the BX when you bought lube and a dozen donuts and asked the poor clerk about proper technique?"

"That was on a dare."

"A dare you won."

He shrugged.

"You *do* know what they're like, though," he insisted.

"Once a year I sit across an enormous boardroom table and drool at those hot, gorgeous, smart, intense men who—hey!"

He pinched her ass.

"I don't need to hear that," he growled.

"You asked," she said in a low, chiding voice. "If you don't want to hear the truth, don't ask."

A slow grin spread across his face. "I'd forgotten that about you."

213

"What? My pinchable ass?" She rubbed the spot where he'd zinged her.

"No. *That* I could never forget." His feelings deepened. "You tell the truth. Always. But you also face it."

"Can't live any other way, Gerald."

His entire body tensed, like a stadium of sports fans doing the wave, one muscle at a time, in sequence. It was a slow motion shiver.

"I know. It's what captivates me."

"It scares the hell out of most men."

"I'm not most men."

"No," she said, in a voice that was half sigh, half regret. "You're not."

"Don't sound so happy about it."

"You ruined me for other men."

"I'm sorry."

She shrugged. The gesture seemed intended to be casual, but it broke something inside him.

His hands slid up from her shoulder to cup her jaw.

"I wish I'd understood back then how your unflinching willingness to face the truth in any situation could have saved us."

"It *would* have saved us."

"And I'll regret not connecting that to reality for the rest of my life."

"I don't want your regrets about the past, Gerald. I want you here. Now. In the present. And I want to talk about how we're going to be in the future. Together."

"C'mon, Suz. Don't be shy. Tell me how you're really feeling." He kissed her then, an awkward, sudden move that she broke, eyes blazing.

"You always used to do that."

"Do what?"

"Cover up talking about feelings with sex."

"Sex *is* a feeling."

Her eyebrows shot up, then curled down, like a silky beige caterpillar being tickled. "What?"

"Sex is a feeling," he insisted. "It's how I express feelings."

"I want you to express your feelings with your mouth."

He began to crawl under the covers, prowling toward her body. "Yes, ma'am...."

"Gerald!" He could hear the laugh in her voice as she struggled to stay serious. Soon, though, she stopped.

This *was* serious.

He needed to have as much of him touching her, and not just through sex. The affinity they shared transcended the pain he'd caused her, the confusion he'd lived through, the emotional muck and mire of so many years lost. As he kissed her, so many thoughts raced through his mind, most of them fragmented and nonsensical, soon replaced by instinct, by touch, neurons firing as he used his hands to find her, to find them.

The feel of her hands on his hip, curving around to find a better grip, the sharp sound of his reaction, the dull blade of need inside making the wound of separation bleed a little more. All these pieces of pain co-existed inside him, shards of himself he'd collected over the years, tossed in a small bag he wore on his back.

As she smoothed his skin, kissed his abs, slid her cheek along the thickening thatch of hair on his belly, he found himself dropping the bag, wondering why he ever needed to carry it at all.

Lighter now, carried off by the wind, he crashed into her and they traveled so high, where no one could see them, above the clouds, his body over hers, her legs around him again, his mouth on hers, the boundary between them gone.

Just air.

And then they closed that gap, too, until the only barrier left was one that only time could dissipate.

She came with a quiet sound of pleasure, her openness so sweet, his own finish one of excitement, their bodies well worn after spending the night together but his thirst for her unquenched. Suzanne was luminous, cheeks pink, eyes wide and searching.

"I love you."

"I never stopped loving you," he said, giving her a tiny piece of herself back, one he'd withheld from that bag of shards.

"Thank you."

The light shining through the cream-colored sheets made her body take on a matte finish, her skin being played with by the light as if she were a toy for amusement. Rays and particles danced in concert to find the most beautiful arrangement of bisecting points and angles, lines and slope. Her body was a mathematical equation, a calculus problem to solve with his hands, his mouth, his body.

His heart and soul.

Computing the area under a curve required deep study.

Very deep.

So deep you lost yourself.

And never wanted to find your way out.

216

Chapter Fifteen

"I can't believe it's been eight weeks already," Agnes complained. "And there aren't any more classes for three weeks!"

"We need the holiday break, Agnes. People are busy shopping and visiting relatives," Gerald explained for the umpteenth time. Suzanne helped to deliver new balls of clay to students, taking in the class.

"Tell that to my kids. Ungrateful little worms. I split myself open how many times, only to have them all move across the country. They don't call." As she watched, Suzanne marveled at the depths of the old lady's cantankerous personality. When she was ninety-something, she wanted to be just like Agnes.

"You Facetime every day with your grandkids in Kentucky, Agnes," her friend, Corrine, corrected. "And your grandson is in college in Boston. He's at your house every weekend." Corrine looked like one of those young women who guest-starred on that old '70s show, *The Love Boat*. A blonde model/actress known only for a few years back then. Suzanne had watched the show with her grandparents on cable, and she struggled to remember the name.

"That's only because I bake cookies for him," Agnes complained.

"I'm sure he visits to enjoy your sunny disposition," Gerald said with a smile, giving Suzanne a wink. "And for your oregano."

Agnes stuck her tongue out at him.

"That's a wrap!" Gerald announced as Declan slipped into his robe, the class standing and applauding.

Declan took a bow, a sweeping gesture of unbridled arrogance that made Gerald burst into hearty laughter.

If you've got it, flaunt it.

"Encore, encore!" Lindi shouted, her dutiful menopause fan whirring away.

Declan whipped off the bathrobe.

Women swooned.

Including Suzanne.

Gerald walked across the room and placed his hand over her eyes.

"Hey!"

"You don't need to look at that."

"Why not?"

"I've got a better view for you at home tonight."

"Better than that?" The room had turned into whistles and sighs.

"Absolutely."

"You'll need to have something mighty special up your sleeve to top that."

"I can top *you*."

"That just sounded wrong, Gerald."

He shrugged. "Blame Andrew McCormick. The guy has some of the worst pick-up lines you could ever imagine."

She shuddered. "Oh, I can imagine."

"He tried to date you, didn't he?"

"How did you know? I mean, he's a nice guy, but totally not my type."

Wincing, Gerald gave her a look. "Of course he isn't. And Declan told me."

"WHAT? When?"

"When we were playing pool that first night you crashed my class."

"Was that really just eight weeks ago?"

218

He kissed the tip of her nose. "It was."

"Did he bring it up on *your* shot?"

"As a matter of fact, he did."

"Who's the *real* pool shark?"

A string of students slowly made their way out of class, stopping to give him a hug or shake his hand. Stacy helped the women with their projects, many of which were perfectly reasonable for brand-new sculpting students. A few stood out.

"Does Declan go by the nickname 'tripod'?" Agnes asked as she eyed Lindi's sculpture.

"AGNES!" Gerald scolded.

She smirked. "See you in three weeks, Mr. Clean!"

Suzanne rubbed his head.

"You know I hate that."

"Then grow it out."

"I hate having hair. Lifting is so much harder."

"Please? For me?"

"Really? Why?"

"It's hard to explain."

"No need. I'll do it. But I have to warn you—there's got to be a ton of grey in there."

"Grey? You're not old enough for grey!"

"Did you get your first grey pube yet?" Corrine asked with that cheerful tone that belied her inappropriateness. "Because once you find one, they're like termites. The colony is already there, just buried where you can't see it."

"BALLS!" Declan declared, coming out of the dressing room and clapping his hands once for emphasis. "Time to play."

Three eager women turned around, offering themselves silently for whatever he was talking about.

"Pool, ladies," Gerald said, motioning for them to leave. "We're playing pool."

"And not pocket pool!" Agnes croaked out from the hall.

"Marie invited you to her yoga class, didn't she? Offered you all the free classes you want?" he asked Gerald, eyeing Corrine's back as she left as if he were tracking her as a dangerous subject.

"Yes." Gerald and Suzanne shared a confused look.

"Don't do it. It's a trap."

"How bad could it be?"

"We can talk about your mother-in-law's yoga class or we can get down to playing with balls," Suzanne declared. "Which is it?"

"Can you lock up, Stacy?" Gerald asked, tossing her the keys to the building. Suzanne knew there were other volunteers in the building who would help.

The teen was ecstatic to be given such a heavy responsibility. "Sure, Gerald! Thanks!"

Five minutes later, at the bar, Suzanne brought back drinks while Gerald glared at Declan.

"Ready?" Declan asked.

Gerald's eyes narrowed as he watched Declan rack the balls. Suzanne held back a snicker, knowing what was coming.

"Yeah. Double or nothing, Mr. Matchmaker."

Laughter poured out of Declan. "You figured it out?"

"Your father told us."

"I thought you needed to see her." Suzanne arched one eyebrow at the guy, but stayed quiet.

"Okay, Marie."

"That's a nasty, low blow," Declan hissed, deferring to Gerald with a gesture that said he could take the first break shot.

"So's interfering with my love life."

"Blame Shannon."

"Shannon?"

"Yes?" To Suzanne's surprise, a young woman stepped from behind Declan, her hands on his shoulders as she planted a kiss on the back of his neck. She had to stand on tiptoes to do it.

Declan spun around and kissed her on the lips. "Shannon! What are you doing here? I thought you were still out of town."

"I tried to make it in time to see you showing off your dangly bits—"

"My bits do not *dangle*. They hang gracefully. They're so graceful because they are *well hung*."

"Mmm hmm." Shannon did not look convinced. The smile she shot Gerald was genuine. "Hey, you! I've missed you."

As he gave her a big hug, she giggled, catching Suzanne's eye.

"You get used to seeing someone most days, and then they're gone. You must not miss some of the crazy errands we sent you on, though."

"Errands?" Suzanne asked, putting a possessive arm around Gerald's waist as she finished her first beer.

"Suzanne, this is Shannon McCormick. Shannon, meet Suzanne Dayton." The two shook hands, though Suzanne kept her fingertips on Gerald's back.

"I've heard your name before, but we've never met," Shannon said to Suzanne. "Declan filled me in on your story. Small world," she said, eyes twinkling.

"Very small," Gerald said. "Matchmaker."

"I just suggested." She looked as disingenuous as she sounded.

As Suzanne watched her boyfriend chat with his old boss's wife, a glow of contentment filled her. Or maybe it was the beer.

Didn't matter.

"Hey," Gerald whispered in Suzanne's ear. "How about we go over to my place tonight and you pose for me?"

"Pose?" She played coy. "Whatever do you mean?"

"I need a nude model."

She pointed to Declan. "You have one."

He squeezed her ass. "I need you."

"You've got me."

"Can you sit very, very still for long periods of time while I memorize your naked body?"

"It'll take a lot of training on my part," she said in a sultry voice. "Might take many, many hours. With hands-on lessons."

"Hands-on, huh?"

"The only way to learn."

THE END

Pre-order *Shopping for a Highlander*, the next book in the Shopping series, now!

I'm a professional c*&^ blocker.

I get paid to follow a womanizing troglodyte who thinks rules are for other people and that my pants are the next pair he's getting into.

Dream on.

Bet your first job out of college didn't involve babysitting an extremely hot, muscle-bound Scottish Highlander with an ego the size of a kilt and a libido bigger than his...well...

Keeping football (that's 'soccer" to us Americans) player Hamish McCormick

away from sex scandals while he does product endorsement campaigns is my mission.

No problem.

Until Hamish decides I'm his next scandal.

And maybe more....

Shopping for a Highlander is a standalone in the New York Times bestselling Shopping for a Billionaire series by Julia Kent. You do not have to have read the previous books, though after you read about Amy and Hamish, you'll want to. ;)

Shopping for a Highlander

* * *

Shopping for a Highlander is coming spring 2017. Join my newsletter mailing list or Facebook page to stay tuned for release dates.

SHOPPING FOR AN HEIR

If you haven't read Declan and Shannon's story in the *Shopping for a Billionaire Boxed Set,* go read it right now! This series began in May 2014 as a serial, and the boxed set has 670+ pages of their hilarious, hot, and crazy story.

Shopping for a Billionaire Boxed Set

OTHER BOOKS BY JULIA KENT

SUGGESTED READING ORDER

SHOPPING FOR AN HEIR

Suspiciously Obedient
Deliciously Obedient

About the Author

Text JKentBooks to 77948 and get a text message on release dates!

New York Times and USA Today bestselling author Julia Kent turned to writing contemporary romance after deciding that life is too short not to have fun. She writes romantic comedy with an edge, and new adult books that push contemporary boundaries. From billionaires to BBWs to rock stars, Julia finds a sensual, goofy joy in every book she writes, but unlike Trevor from *Random Acts of Crazy*, she has never kissed a chicken.

She loves to hear from her readers by email at jkentauthor@gmail.com, on Twitter @jkentauthor, and on Facebook at facebook.com/jkentauthor

Visit her website at http://jkentauthor.com